The Crack in the Sun
novel

Monte Jaffe

Published 2022

Herstellung und Verlag: BoD – Books on Demand,

Norderstedt

ISBN: 9783756835140

FSC
www.fsc.org

MIX
Papier aus verantwortungsvollen Quellen
Paper from responsible sources
FSC® C105338

About the author

Monte Jaffe began writing in Chattanooga, Tennessee, where he was born, composing songs and writing short stories and TV scripts.

He supported the civil rights movement, working and living with the Highlander Folk Group, followers of Martin Luther King.

He later moved to New York, going underground to avoid being drafted into the Vietnam War. He did roofing and construction work and worked as a social worker in the notorious Hell's Kitchen. Echoes of these challenges reverberate through the pages of his novels.

In 1982 he moved to Europe, pursuing a successful career singing opera. Presently he lives with his wife in northern Germany.

Visit him on www.montejaffe.com and www.montejaffe.de

CHAPTER 1

This guy's running as fast as he can. His name is Max Fagan. Organized crime is after him. Three muscular fat guys with iron pipes and handguns are running after him and laughing. They're having fun because their adrenaline is up. In a way the whole chase is doing Max good too. It's taking his mind off his problems. Max is a carrier. In a certain world, you can't write checks. Money is transferred in light brown paper bags by ex-boxers, like Lewis Brown, who have been knocked into eternal innocence and are therefore totally trustworthy; or actor types, like Max, looking to make a little extra cash by doing non-judgmental errands. These guys are called carriers.

Max ducks into a bar where the rules don't allow the fat guys to go, territorial sensitivity (they were just having fun anyway), and he looks for the recipient of the light brown bag. The owners of this bar didn't waste money on décor, which is a kind of décor. Atmosphere is a result rather than a planned goal, and there is plenty of atmosphere, naked ladies dancing on the bar top, not gorgeous drop-dead beauties, just normal, mildly interesting young women, mostly students, walking around naked on the bar and letting themselves be stared at. The recipient of the brown bag is actually a Jewish guy, white hair, thin, around sixty and if his grandchildren could see him now, all dressed in black leather, well, we all have our needs. Max

1

gives the bag to Zorro Finkelstein, who puts it in a safe. The young actor says good night and leaves. Back out on Tenth Ave., Max looks around to make sure he is alone, along with the other millions of residents of midtown Manhattan, and he is.

The question now is, where will Max sleep tonight? Maybe Marylyn's. He met her while walking down the street mumbling lines from a play he was memorizing. The words were, "She was untouched, oh Lord. She was untouched before her young body was defiled by my hands, defiled by my lust." These mumbled words caused a look in Marylyn's eyes that promised a future for the mumbler and the young woman. While explaining the reason for his utterances, Max became involved in an evening of dinner at her place (he didn't have one), rump steak with lots of Worcestershire sauce and Rioja wine, social worker talk (that was her profession) and interesting sex, because, among other things, she peed when she came, which was warm.

Max could also stay at Marco's, which was uptown at 148th St. in Spanish Harlem. Always a corner place there; or down at Ellen's in the Village. It's not that he doesn't have money. He has lots of jobs, under the table money jobs. It is simply that this is his time of running. People have running times. Wars cause running times, private and world wars, but also running can be the result of the inner furnace, the burning off of the carbon in search of the diamond. It will be Marco's tonight. It's late. So it's up to Harlem. He hops a subway and heads uptown.

Sitting in the uptown local at twelve at night can cause thoughts to gather in the mind. Most normal people have organized themselves to sleep or at least to a resting-place. People who are not so organized, the populations of the restless, often find themselves in subways at this late hour, moving on to their next stop before they reach nowhere in particular.

Max decided to stop off at the Oasis first. It's just a few doors down from Marco's apartment. He'll stop in first for a quick check-in drink, before going to Marco's. Maybe Jose will be there. Jose is a short man of color. Max is white, so normally the Oasis is off limits. It's not a bar for everybody. Max had met Jose one morning outside Marco's place. Jose had seemed just to be standing around. People do that in Harlem. They have their place on the street, and they just hang around there. It's like their office. Certain times of the day you can always find them there, talking with friends, whatever. Max saw Jose just standing around, so Max just let the vibes happen. Harlem functions on vibes. They seemed good. Max and Jose started up a conversation. It turned out that Jose hadn't been just standing around. In his pocket he had a buzzer. There was some gambling going on in the basement of Marco's building, gambling and numbers. Every few minutes a guy would go down the stairs to the basement entrance, and Jose would buzz him in. All this was going on while Max was chatting with Jose, and Max didn't even notice it. Max didn't have street eyes. Jose just told Max what he was doing, by way of educating him to street ways. It was an act of friendship and trust. Max felt honored. Another time, Max was walking up Broadway on his way to Marco's, and Jose bumped into him and lifted his wallet. Max didn't feel a thing. Jose handed the wallet back to Max and showed him how he had done it. Max would learn a lot from Jose. Out of gratitude, Max invited Jose to dinner. Jose was surprised.

"No one has ever taken me to dinner before."

It was a strange thing for Max to hear. Everyone has been invited to a meal sometime or another. They went to a soul food restaurant around the corner and had a great Southern feast. After the meal they walked by the Oasis.

Max joked, "If I were to go in that bar, I'd never come out alive."

"You want to go into that bar? Let's go in. I'll buy you a drink."

"You know they won't let me in that bar."

"You're with me, man. Let's go."

That's how Max got into the Oasis.

Getting out of the subway at 145th, Max goes up Broadway toward the Oasis. He loves this part of town, Spanish and Cuban music coming from portable radios, people walking down the street laughing, having a good time. The night air is alive.

He enters the Oasis wearing a shirt of many flowers, which makes him just a little bit more welcome than otherwise and is not greeted but is not thrown out. They don't bother with mixed drinks at the Oasis, so he orders Jack Daniel's straight. Jose is not there. Against the back wall, some sitting on stools, some standing, is the gallery of drug-addicted young beauties. Out of respect (and that is the secret word) you don't smile at them, that would mean business, and you don't look judgmental, that would mean trouble. The big, very well-dressed guys next to them look at you to see if there is any action, and if there is not, then what the hell are you doing here; but that's your business. One custom-made suit guy comes over and asks if Max has change for a ten, which means something else other than if you have change for a ten, and Max says no, and the suit man goes away. Max is beginning to feel very white. A man comes over to him and starts speaking Spanish. Max smiles.

"Sorry, I don't speak Spanish."

The man is very drunk. He has pissed in his pants, but could care less.

He mumbles, "What you speak?"

"French. Je parle français."

As luck would have it, so did the drunk, Caribbean French.

"Je vais te tuer. I will kill you."

Max smiled and asked, "Comment tu feras cela? How are you going to do

it?" trying to keep his verbs straight.

"Avec ça. With this."

The drunk pulls a pistol out of his pocket. Within seconds six men grab the drunk Caribbean. It had seemed that no one had been paying any attention to their conversation, but in the Oasis everybody pays attention to everything. They disarm him, push him outside and come back in as if nothing has happened. Max stands alone at the bar.

"What's happenin', man?"

It was Jose. Max was very glad to see him.

"I was just about shot. That's what's happenin'. How you doin'?"

"Ain't nobody gonna shoot you here, man."
Jose is not a big man. He's not into any drug action. Nothing about him seems dangerous. He certainly isn't rich, but he is highly respected in the neighborhood. He has a room somewhere, but he doesn't have a phone as far as Max knows. He has an ex-wife who is a prison guard in some Women's Detention Institute. He told Max he had laid a man flat once.
"What's that?"
Jose explained.

"I killed him."
He didn't say it with pride or guilt or anything. He said it by way of educating Max, translating street language. Jose knew the street. It was his world. In his world he was just a normal guy. He said if Max ever needed anything, he would get it for him. Max didn't need anything Jose could get. Not yet, anyway.

Max leaves the Oasis and heads up to Marco's. He looks at his watch and notices that it is almost three, a little late to wake Marco up, so where? If you're gonna wake somebody up, then maybe Marylyn. She's warm and has a woman's understanding about these things. He'll call first.

"Hello, Marylyn. Max. You sleeping? Dumb question. You want a drink?"

"Max? What time is it? You want to come over? I'll buzz you in, but I got to sleep. Come on over."
Max sleeps at Marylyn's that night.

Well, that's one day in Max's life, actually half a day. You multiply this times three hundred and whatever it is, and you have a year, and Max has lots of years ahead of him with no idea what the hell will happen next.

Max wakes up the next morning. The bed's not wet. Marylyn doesn't always pee. She has gone to work. He remembers kissing her good morning as she took off and then rolling over for a few more hours of sleep. So, morning in this bed, Marylyn's bed, Marylyn's place. He gets up and makes himself a cup of coffee. Women have nice homes, little decorations around, flowers, interesting art pictures hanging on the walls and a bookcase full of books. He's in her private domain, a sexy feeling, alone in Marylyn's apartment. He could look through her drawers, panties and things. That would be an invasion somehow. He takes a long, slow bath. That's not an invasion. He cleans up his traces like a good Indian and goes out, back on the street, cold October street.

Max walks toward the City Library. He really didn't have to hurry like the people around him were hurrying. He enjoyed his aimlessness and was also a little frightened by it. People all around him were on their way somewhere. They had that look on their face that everything will be OK when they get to where they are going. Max looked at a reflection of himself in a store window and put on a serious face, full of purpose. Then he laughed because he looked like an idiot. He did have a place to go—the library. He just had a lifetime to get there.

Max thought about his parents wandering around in New York many years ago, before they finally settled in Chattanooga, Tennessee. He thought about them getting off the boat from Europe and wandering around with no place to go, looking at themselves in the store window reflections. They were probably still thin. Their winter coats were probably like tents around them. They were camp survivors, Dachau. Max's grandparents had left Europe before it had been too late to leave, and they had settled in Chattanooga, Tennessee, so that's where Max's parents eventually settled, but first Max's parents had wandered the streets of New York, like Max was doing. They had probably been frightened too, but really frightened, not just philosophically frightened like Max. They had probably wondered if they would survive; even though they had survived, they probably wondered if they would survive at least until the next day. They are probably still wondering if they will survive until tomorrow, down there in Chattanooga, Tennessee. Max thought about his parents wandering around on the sidewalks he was now wandering around on.

What's up today? He's got to make a run for Lew later. Lew is the ex-boxer who usually does the brown bag runs for Abe, the porno man, but Lew is having his eyes lifted. He's in his early fifties and is still very strong. He's seeing a 'younger woman' and is concerned about his beat up face. Actually it's a great face, but even ex-boxers can be insecure. His eyes do have a squinty look. One would think that would be advantageous in bedroom matters, but what do I know? Anyway, Lew is recovering from his eyelift, so Max is taking over his run for a while. The money is going from Abe to Zorro for services rendered. Don't ask.

Max will go over to Abe's love nest suite later and get the bag. But it's around eleven now, plenty of time. He's got to go somewhere now, where he can study the scene he's working on for acting class. He's working on a scene from 'Darkness at Noon' with his scene partner, Shurbe.

It would be nice to have a place of his own.

He had shared an apartment with Diane for a while, but they broke up. She wanted someone with more money. Who could blame her? Also, in all honesty, he had a wandering eye. He moved out. First he went to Marco's, took a few things with him, then spent some time at Ellen's. Ellen is an older actress, more of a mother-friend who had survived the McCarthy era. He has a few things there too. Anyway, he sort of drifted into drifting, but soon he should get a room somewhere.

'Darkness at Noon' and Shurbe. Shurbe is thin, blond and very courageous. She had been in a mental institution, haven't we all. They were giving her cool out pills, and one day she threw them in the toilet and walked out the door. She had gone in voluntarily and gone out voluntarily, only to discover that she was not an elephant in a porcelain store, she was porcelain in an elephant world. She and Max worked well together. They did several scenes for the class and several scenes for themselves. Max spent some time with her, but she said that living with him was like playing tennis uphill. She eventually moved far away and then again, not so far.

There is a special bookstore for theatre books on 50th, just off Broadway. Max goes there to get the 'Darkness At Noon' script, then he heads up to the Lincoln Center library to read the play. He meets Shurbe at five, they rehearse a while, then he goes to pick up the bag.

One of the clowns in God's tent of characters is Abe, the porno man. Abe is not in the porno business per se. Actually he has a house on Long Island and a wife and two kids. He just owns the buildings where the porn occurs. On the other hand, Abe is a perfect porn person. He is slob fat, but that is just the beginning. He has a physical condition, maybe caused by a nerve disorder, whereby his tongue always hangs out over his lower lip. He also usually has a cigar stuck in the remaining mouth space. All this affects his speech. So when Max goes over to make the pick up, the occasion usually turns into a study of human triumph over obstacles such as reality and acceptable good taste. Max rings the penthouse doorbell. By the way, Abe also owns the building where the penthouse is. First Max hears Abe waddling to the door, then security noises, looking through the hole in the door which makes everyone look funny, unlocking many locks, heavy breathing, then the inevitable,

"Whoth there?"

Eventually Abe opens the door, and Max is let into an oxygen-free apartment. The smell of stale cigar smoke and some other smell alert the visitor's brain that we're dealing with some other kind of human being. Max is then led through several rooms that were never used for anything other than a passageway to the bedroom. The bedroom has a water-bed, with mirrors over the bed, green, drawn curtains and a green bedspread. The breathing factor in this room is inhibited by a stench coming from colognes and sexual labor, all several hours or several months old. Abe reports,

"Lath night I had two cunth in thith bed. Futh them both in the ath."

Abe gives Max the bag and gives new dimension to vulgarity.

The city condemned some buildings on East 93rd, the old Rupert Brewery tenement houses. The plan was to tear down the buildings and build apartment houses, but it would be about a year, maybe two, before the tenement houses would be torn down. In the meantime, you could rent apartments called railroad flats for very little money. Max heard about the apartments through some actor friends and found himself a home. He painted the ceiling sky blue, with some sand in the paint to give it a cloudy look. His apartment was on the top floor, which was great, because it was near the rooftop of the building. The rooftop of a tenement house was special. You could spend time up there thinking and drinking a beer like it was a penthouse terrace. He lived there for about two years.

Max brought Mimi there and tried to live with her. It was a blissful catastrophe. Mimi couldn't speak English. She only spoke French, which was OK because Max spoke French, but Mimi couldn't speak to anyone other than Max except for very few other people. That was also OK, because Mimi wasn't very gregarious. She just liked to lay around and read and eat delicious food She was a specialist in love making, like a courtesan, except she didn't do it for money. She just loved to make love. Max met her when he went to Canada for a few weeks that summer. They imploded into each other, and when the pieces settled, she left a relationship in Quebec and came with Max to New York. Luckily he had this apartment in the condemned tenement building he could offer as a home for them. They spent a lot of time making love. Max being temporarily unemployed, time was in abundance. Eventually a train speeding toward a wall will hit the wall unless common sense is brought to bear, and of course, common sense was a language neither one of them spoke. Oh, that was a painful train crash. Her former Quebecian friend drove down and picked her up and drove away with her. Max's whirlwind life whirled on.

Max was out of work, so he called up the Dressers Union. Maybe there was some extra work on Broadway or at the Met. He was supposed to call a certain Mary Jones. She knew about job openings. Mary wasn't there, so somebody took Max's name and phone number down and left them on Mary's desk. That's why his name and phone number was there on her desk when a famous actor called and said that his dresser had dropped dead and he needed a new dresser. Mary looked down and saw Max's name and phone number and sent Max over to meet the famous actor to see if the chemistry worked. It did, and Max was employed.

What a dresser did was not really clear to Max. He had been helped by a dresser when he performed. A dresser held the jacket or pants as Max slipped out of one costume and into another. But more than that Max didn't know. So he would learn.

Aside from caring for the costumes, hanging them up after the show, seeing that they were cleaned etc., Max's other main job was to make sure the bar was always well stocked. Cutty Sark and Guinness stout were the main staples. The famous actor drank a roaring lot. So did his famous colleague. With her it was champagne or 'champs', as she called it, but that was *her* dresser's problem.

Her dresser was a gloriously heavy, black woman named Besulda. Besulda had a voice that came out of a huge heart filled with centuries of explosive living. She also had a hollow wooden leg and could outdrink even these heavy weights. Max was a young robin in this area, drinking booze from a booze puddle while admiring the great ocean guzzlers. There was a third somewhat famous actor in the play, 'Country Girl'. He was a quieter type. So Max swam among the whales. It was lively.

The show opened in Washington, and all the Washington people tried to outdo each other giving parties for the famous. Max and Besulda were more or less a necessary evil for these party hosts. They weren't famous, and they ate and drank a lot, but the famous actor and the famous actress wouldn't dream of Max and Besulda not being a part of the festivities. And the one thing you didn't want to do was to offend this particular actor. He could get pretty angry.

There was one short but memorable rage that occurred at the closing night party of the Washington run. It was about three in the morning, and the house was filled with theatre people unloading the last buckets of energy before moving on to the next project or period of uncertainty. The actor had called a friend in Ireland. The friend didn't want to come to the phone. This enraged the actor who began to curse his ex-friend; ex-until morning, when reality exchanged places with booze. The actor poured waves of violent raging into the living room, causing one innocent lovely to cry. Max quickly came to her aid. Everyone mumbled good night and left—one guy through a window, which was open anyway. Max and the actor were alone in the living room. Max, somewhat amused with the drama, his own perspective heavily ingratiated with sprits, stood next to the actor and watched the show. Then he offered the actor a drink. Timing is everything. They sat down and finished off a bottle of Cutty Sark and discussed a new project the actor was considering, where Max could play an important role. The project was a play called 'The Dresser'. The dresser would be played by Max. Oh booze, how splendid is thy lie. Around 8:00 Max remembered he had a train to catch back to New York. So he said goodbye to the actor, "Thanks for the party," and got a taxi to his hotel where he threw anything that looked like it might be his into a suitcase and checked out of the hotel.

He took another taxi to an alabaster train station where Besulda was desperately looking for him because she had his ticket, and the train was about to leave. Max stood swaying among hundreds of people. He knew he had very little time, so he took a short cut. He went to the middle of the alabaster station, where the acoustics were the best and called in a somewhat scotchy voice,

"Besulda!"

From some far corner, he heard the unmistakable voice of Besulda's reply,

"There you is! Honey, we gots to hurry".

She grabbed him, and put him on the train, and that is how he got back to New York.

When he arrived at Grand Central, he hailed a cab up to 200th Street where he lived with Bunny at that time. Bunny was a beautiful woman with creamy black skin, warm brown eyes and an exquisite body. The only endearing imperfection she had was one of her fingers. Her mother had had a fondness for chalk during pregnancy, and one of Bunny's fingers was a little crooked because of too much calcium. Bunny would have made a great life partner for Max, but Max was burning carbon. She eventually went to Switzerland and married some rich doctor. But when Max poured into their apartment on 200th, they were glad to see each other, in fact, so glad that after some champagne and tenderness, they went to Marco's, who was giving a little party. Max (who, by this time, had been up for two whole days, and had consumed a considerable mixture of alcoholic fluids), came in, greeted his friend and noticed a bottle of vodka. He opened it, poured himself a drink, drank it down and fell on his face.

Max woke up the next day in his room in the corner. This time his collision with the erratic circus of chaotic people hurt. He had a severe pain in his solar plexus. He never drank that much again in his life. It was the end of his journey through the boozy lives of the stars. It was great, but it was over. It wasn't the pain in his solar plexus that turned him off to that life. It was simply the feeling that they were all going on a journey that ended somewhere far away from where Max wanted to go. They were voyagers too, like Max, and Max loved the feeling of the ride, oh yes, the riding was thrilling, and it's not that Max knew where the hell he was headed, but the demons in Max's ass were just different demons. The famous actor and actress had theirs and Max had his. Max saw the actor a few years later in a play on Broadway. He went backstage and said hello. The actor had had a serious auto accident and had given up drink, but there was a champagne glass filled with light tan liquid sitting on his make-up table. Max didn't know if he later drank it—a one-glass reward for work well done—or if it was just a reminder of a journey he used to be on. Max and the actor parted and Max never saw him again except occasionally on a late night movie on TV.

CHAPTER 2

Max continued his journey through his house of mirrors. Every mirror he looked into seemed cracked. An opera singer in his acting class wanted to sing Violetta in the opera, 'La Traviata'. The singer had access to some money to produce the opera at the Providence Town Playhouse in the Village and wanted to know if Max would direct it. Max wasn't sure where she got the money to produce an opera and didn't ask. The singer, a robust blonde with cobalt blue eyes, by the name of Sandy Sandinsky would of course sing the role of Violetta. The main roles were to be double casted, so they held auditions. That's how Max met Chrystal.

The auditions were held at the Providence Town Playhouse. It was a small theater, seated about five hundred. Max and Sandy sat in the back as the singers came on to audition. A beautiful young woman came to the center of the stage and announced that her name was Chrystal Bergmann.

Chrystal seemed, in many ways, the opposite of Sandy. Sandy was rough. Chrystal was not rough at all. She seemed quiet. She seemed to have an active inner life. When she began to sing, it was a slow disrobing of her secrets. Max felt honored to be in attendance to her tenderness, her willingness.

"Miss Bergmann, you have a lovely voice. Have you sung the role of Violetta?"

"Thank you. Yes, I mean, I've sung some scenes from Traviata in a workshop."

"How do you see her? Why did she lose? Why was she the victim?"

"She lived in an illusion. I see her as a child playing with life, but no one had the guts to play on her level of innocence. At one point she notices that she is alone. The loneliness becomes an illness. When the right partner comes along, she is too deep in her illness to recover."

"Why doesn't she see the problem coming? Why doesn't she protect herself?"

"She knew she was dying. From the beginning of the opera she knew she was dying. In a way that's what made her lonely life bearable, that it would end. Her only protection was her childlike innocence. She would rather keep her innocence, her child trust, than grow up and become like the adults around her."

Chrystal was offered the role.

After high school Chrystal had attended a private college in upstate New York. There were a few men students, but mostly it was a college for young women with intellectual ambitions in a broad range of fields, a little music, a little art, a little fashion design. There was a lot of theory and conversation, but there was not a lot of genuine talent or experience in the real world. When she graduated, she considered going to Paris or maybe getting into theater in New York. She had had enough theory and intellectual bullshit. She was hungry for the real thing.

She found a voice teacher in New York and took acting classes from an important acting teacher. When she had heard about the Traviata production, she decided to audition. Getting the role felt good, felt right. This guy Max seemed OK, seemed like a no-bullshit guy. The rehearsals took place in Sandy's large living room on 84th street. Max seemed to have a clear idea about what he was after.

"This opera is about the danger of illusion. All the characters live in a world of lies they have made up so they can get through the day. Their festivities are not really festive, and their love is bought and paid for."

The rehearsals went pretty late. One night after a rehearsal, Max walked with Chrystal to the subway.

"It was a good rehearsal, Chrystal. It's coming along. I'm hungry. You want a bite?"

"Sure."

They went to a diner on Broadway. Max held a cup of black coffee between his palms to get his hands warm. It was a cold autumn night.

"Chrystal, I like what you are doing very much, almost too much. I get the feeling that you are comfortable with Violetta's life, you accept it, just take its journey where it leads you."

"Max, what are you telling me? You don't like it?"

"I like it. I like it. Do you think she resists the journey, accepts it, but also fights it?"

"Why would she fight it? It's her life. Just raise hell and die. That's who she is."

"What if she found a cure, got free from the shit around her ?"

"That's the point, she can't, and she knows it, so she goes for it one hundred percent. That's what I like about her."

"I think that's what I like about you. I don't think that's what I like about Violetta."

"But Max, life *is* an illusion. We all have dreams to help us ward off fears, our insecurities."

"Fine, but what good are they if we wake up dead? Where do you live?"

"In the Village. You?"

"On 99th. Can you get home OK?"

"You don't like what I'm doing?"

"I think you are magnificent."

"That's not what I asked."

"Chrystal, I'm just a director. I just watch, and I love watching you, listening to you."

"You're smooth Max, smooth."

"I think about people who really have no hope, really know that they are going to die. I wonder what they think, what goes on in their minds. I think some of them accept their fate, and some resist it. The ones who resist it are heroes. I think Violetta is a hero."

"Who do you think about, Max? What people? It's late. We'll talk tomorrow."

"May I buy you some coffee?"

"No thanks. See you tomorrow."

Chrystal left, and Max held the coffee cup to warm his hands. Chrystal went home and Max went home, and something of each stayed with each.

The rehearsal the next evening started with Sandy. Sandy was great. She was a kind of Mae West character, eighteen going on forty. It seems she was being supported by some mysterious sugar daddy. She also took trips to Miami on occasion, the guest of some wealthy elderly gentleman, but she was mainly her sugar daddy's geisha, and it was sugar daddy who was footing the Traviata project. Sandy had known the guy for quite some time. Max didn't ask too many questions, but it was clear that sugar daddy wanted to stay very much in the background. It also turned out that Lewis Brown, Max's old brown bag partner, was Sandy's uncle, and Lew showed up from time to time to help with set building and with rounding up props. The whole thing was turning out to be a family affair supported by a Jewish mafia. Max could care less. He was interested in two things, Traviata and Chrystal Bergmann.

It was Chrystal's turn to rehearse.

"Chrystal, let's do the first aria. The guests have gone and you are alone. You've met this guy Alfredo, and in a year or so you'll be dead, TB."

"I know all that, Max."

"I want to try something. Imagine you'll sing the aria, then after it you'll be taken out and be executed, shot."

"How could I sing if that were the case?"

"How could you not sing? You're a singer. If you were a religious Jew, you'd say the Sh'ma Israel. If you were a Catholic, you would say the rosary. It's your time, the end of your time, yours to do with what you want."

Max nodded to the pianist.

"Music!"

The pianist started the intro. Chrystal began to sing. Tears and fury filled her face and her voice. She hated Max. She fell to her knees and continued singing through her anger and tears. When she finished she was on her knees sobbing. Max went to her and put his arms around her.

"Now, you're a heroine, Chrystal."

"I hate you, Max."

She put her arms around him and kissed him. That was the end of rehearsing. Thoughts quit. They walked toward the subway.

"Let's go to my apartment."

"Yes."

They went to Max's. It was nearer. Their passion was urgent, and then they didn't talk. They didn't think about anything, they spoke with breathing and with gentle touching, then they came again with each other, again, and then they slept.

The next morning it was wonderful to be next to each other. They spent the morning naked, drinking coffee and feeling natural. Max made breakfast, bacon and eggs. They were hungry. Chrystal stood next to Max in the kitchen.

"So much for not having an affair."

"Is this an affair?"

"I don't know what this is. Where does Sandy get the money to do this production? Is she rich?"

"Sugar daddy."

"Who is he?"

"No idea. The production, the apartment. I think they've known each other a long time."

"Do you think he's a gangster or something?"

"I think Lew, the guy who shows up sometimes with sandwiches and coffee, I think he works for this sugar daddy. Lew and I used to transport little brown paper bags of money for him, money that wasn't traceable. Porno money."

"Are you into porno?"

"No. A few years ago I did a few errands with Lew. Harmless stuff. No big deal."

"You never met this friend of Sandy's?"
"No, he stays pretty much out of the picture, pulls the strings but keeps a low profile. I just want to direct this opera and make love with you."

"You're not going to end up dead, floating in the river are you?"

"I got away from that bunch. Life is too short."

They put their clothes on and separated, went about their day until that night, until the rehearsal started.

Sunday came, the Christian day of rest. Chrystal and Max had a routine. In the few short weeks, they had established a routine. The routine was simply that they came home, either to hers or to his, together.

"You think a lot about death don't you, Max?"

"Chrystal, what a crazy thing to say."

"You do."

"Fuck death. I don't think about death. I mean, the opera is about death, but today's Sunday."

"Did somebody die, somebody close to you?"

"No. Somebody didn't die, it was close, but no, they didn't die. My parents waited for death like the other shoe falling. It's funny, after a while you want the shoe to fall. Let it fall. Let the fucking shoe fall and get it over with. Boy, you can put a person in a good mood."

"It's a color in your face, a waiting color. Your dream is that death will come any second, and you're released from duty, from some pain. It's in your face, Max, like a crystal glass waiting to break. That's how you knew about Violetta. You saw the glass in my face and you broke it."

"And you want to break mine."

"Yes. I want to break all the illusions separating me from life."

"You have a lot of courage, Chrystal."

"That's what I want to know. Can someone live a simple life without kidding themselves?"

"Jesus Christ, Chrystal, you don't want much, do you?"

"Too much?"

"Only everything. My answer is yes, but it's only an answer in my mind, not in my real life. I can't do it in my real life. Maybe someday. My illusion is that I will do it as an artist, as a lover, a director, a writer, but these are safe dreams, dreams which separate me from danger in case I fail, in case death comes to me one day and laughs at me and tells me I'm just a phony self-deluding bullshit artist, with a way with words but not with living. Then death takes me away, just another self-absorbed, maybe even successful artist, takes me away to rot like every human joke God tells in His night club act we call Creation. In the beginning God told a joke, and the joke was good."

"You sound like Christ on the cross. Why hast Thou forsaken me?"

"He put it better. He was a great poet."

"Did death laugh when it came for Him?"

"Christians say that He laughed at death. I don't blame them. It's a beautiful illusion. But you're not an illusion, Chrystal."

"That's what I wanted to hear.Thank you."

The Province Town Playhouse is an important theater in the history of American theater. It was in this theater that Eugene O'Neill premiered his, at that time, courageous masterpiece, 'All God's Chillun Got Wings'. Max was honored to have his first directorial efforts presented in this very special space. Sandy sang the premiere in her straightforward gutsy style. She portrayed an older woman whose dreams of youth were awakened by a young lover. Her struggle with death was courageous and convincing. A thin man sat in the back of the auditorium. No one saw him come in, and no one saw him leave. Sandy knew he would be there and would leave without coming back to say hello. She was used to that. She didn't mind. He was, after all, the one who made the whole production possible. She'd call him later when she got home, find out what he thought. Sandy met her sugar daddy some twenty years ago, when she was a young beauty with a broad and friendly butt, and he was an immigrant from Germany, come to America to make good, one way or another. Their

25

friendship spanned the years. He was good to her, and she was good to him, but the delicate balance between his generosity and his sudden viciousness caused her to dance a tightrope, a dance she was never sure she would survive. Sandy thrived on danger. She could handle it. She had so far and would continue to.

There are many rewards and frustrations connected with theater. It's a world the world would do well to look at: egos and energies colliding, individuals coming together from different countries, speaking different languages, both psychologically and literally, the perfect set-up for catastrophe, and catastrophe occurs as often as breakfast. Yet, in spite of these tenuous circumstances, the show goes on, almost always. It goes on because all the participants eventually put aside their self-importance in the name of the profession to which they are dedicated. There are occasional glitches in the aforementioned scenario, but rarely. The show almost always goes on. If the world is a stage, and we are mere players, then there is something wrong, because all too often, for many victims in our world play, the show stops, the world doesn't go on.

Some obtain fame and fortune in this profession, but the real reward, the reward which lasts over the years, through the ups and downs, is the friendships which develop among the illusion-makers, the transporters of dreams. And so it was with Sandy and Chrystal. Chrystal was there for Sandy on the opening night to wish good luck, break a leg, and when Chrystal sang her first

Traviata, Sandy was there to wish her well. This friendship lasted as long as they both were alive.

Chrystal's performance was magic. It was not witnessed by thousands of viewers, just a few hundred, but maybe one of them was Verdi. This all sounds romantic and maybe even naive, but that is one of the charms of opera. The willingness to be in touch with a child's trust in fantasy is the price for the ticket to ride, and ride she did. Max was proud of his new love. Their bond grew. Her success as Violetta got her an offer to join the Canadian Opera Touring Company, with 'La Traviata' and 'La Bohème'. Their relationship encountered the test of distance, a test which many theater relationships fail.

The company toured most of Canada and played some of the larger American cities. It lasted about six months. Chrystal wanted Max next to her. She wanted to share what she felt while riding through some of the most beautiful country she had ever seen. After leaving Toronto, the company went westward across the vast snow-covered plains of Saskatchewan and into the ice castle forests of Alaska, then down into British Columbia. She wanted to show Max that it was really their Violetta that she was playing.

The company played the great halls and the school gymnasiums. They played for the social set and for farmers and lumberjacks. She wanted to share all this with Max, which made a few guys in the company pretty jealous, but eat your heart out guys, that's life. One night the company performed for an American Indian reservation. She called after the show.

"Max, it was wonderful! They clapped all night. They had never seen an opera before. I felt like Jenny Lind singing in the Wild West days."

"Don't lose your scalp, Chrystal. I'm pretty fond of it."

"Me too."

"That was just a little cheap of me. I guess I'm a little jealous. Is that all right for me to be a little jealous?"

"I hope you're more than a little jealous."

"When will you get back to New York?"

"We play a few more towns, then we go to San Francisco, then Chicago. After Chicago, it's home. Put some champagne on ice. I'm getting pretty thirsty."

" 'On ice' is the magic word."

"Max, the landscape in this part of the world is not to be believed. It's like nothing I've ever seen, the forests, they're like a sea of never-ending trees, huge waves as large as mountains, ending somewhere in mist and clouds. Come here, Max. Let's just swim forever in the snow sea, keeping each other warm and safe."

"Do you feel safe, Chrystal? Do you feel safe in so much ecstasy? Isn't it scary to feel so much beauty?"

"If I were alone, I couldn't stand it, but I feel that you are very much with me. I tell you things when I'm walking around. The trees must think humans are crazy plants."

"You've got to try some moose meat. See if one of your Native Americans can get you some moose meat."

"I'll bring you moose meat, Max, moose meat and mystery from the Wild West."

"I don't want to scare you away, Chrystal. Sometimes I feel like I'm flying through time, devouring information. I can't get enough of anything. I can't slow down. Then something will stop me, like you, like when you sing, and being still and flying becomes the same thing, and that's when I'm me, really me. I'm afraid that when I'm flying around, it scares people. They like it at first, but then they get angry at my flying, so I fly away. I don't want my flying to scare you, Chrystal."

"I'll fly with you, Max."

"There are auditions for Lear. Some Finnish director, Sven something, down at the Circle in the Square. I want to play Lear."

"Aren't you a little young for Lear?"

"That's part of the concept. They want a young Lear."

"Give it a try. Why not?"

"Audition's tomorrow. I'll tell you about it. I want you here. I want you there. I want you."

"That's the magic word."

Max got the part. It was a weird production, weird concept. Sven Somebody was the director, a guy from Finland. He was one of those self-acclaimed saviors of theatrical destiny. The plan was to destroy the play, cause a scandal and get famous, maybe become a Finnish knight. The whole play took place in a swimming-pool, and Lear was a child molester. Max had to admit that Cordelia looked great in a bathing suit. The interviews were fascinating, and the discussions about artistic freedom, breaking down old barriers, were drenched in narcissistic, modest self-amazement. This kind of bullshit was fashionable and, unfortunately, successful. If you don't understand anything, and it looks 'interesting', then it is a success. Max was trying to stay cool, but it was getting harder and harder. He was walking home from a rehearsal one night, when a prostitute propositioned him.

"Hey, wanna go out?"

Max took a look at her smiling face.

"Did you ever think of playing Lear?"

"No, but you could teach me, baby."

"No, sweetheart, but I bet you could teach me a thing or two."

During the rehearsal the next day, Max found himself thinking about the prostitute. He thought, 'This damn director is trying to make me a prostitute. I'm supposed to act like he's some genius and play along with him. Well, he can fiddle with his own dildo. Fuck him!'

Suddenly he quit fondling Cordelia, and shouted, "This is bullshit!" and walked out.

Finnish Sven was furious and fired him.

Max called Chrystal.

"I just couldn't put up with the bullshit. It felt like prostitution. I'm glad I'm out."

"Max, I'm proud of you. I'm glad you're out too. When I get back, I'll put on a bathing suit, and you can fondle me."

"I wonder who will end up playing Lear, maybe the prostitute."

The touring company played San Francisco. Chrystal was a great success. They moved on to Chicago. It was after a show in Chicago that the tragedy happened.

It was around twelve at night. Chrystal was feeling good. She wanted to get home and call Max. She left the theater and walked quickly towards the hotel where the cast was staying. She quickly said good night to some of her colleagues in the lobby and ran up to her room. When she opened the door to her room, she was suddenly pushed inside. A man was standing above her. She started to scream and the man hit her in the face and she fell unconscious. When she came to, she saw her pants had been ripped off, and she realized that she had been raped. Her vagina was bleeding. She tried to stand. She fell over, grabbing the telephone. She screamed into the telephone, "I've been raped!"
And passed out.

Chrystal comes to the next morning. She is lying in a hospital bed. She feels her face. There is something taped to her face. Her body hurts. A woman is standing looking down at her. The woman's expression is strange, concerned.
"How are you feeling?"
"Who are you?"
"I'm a doctor. How do you feel?"
"Where am I?"
"You're in a hospital. St. Mary's Hospital."

"I have to go. I have to get up. What's this on my face?"

"It's a bandage. You've been hit in the face."

"I've got to get up. I've got to sing tonight. What time is it?"

"Do you know what has happened to you?" Chrystal tries to get up. She notices that she is dressed in a hospital gown.

"Where are my clothes? What time is it?" She falls back on the bed.

"Rest now. Take it easy. You've had a rough time. Do you know what has happened?" Chrystal looks up at the doctor's strange face.

"I've been raped." She passes out.

Max waited to hear from Chrystal. He was getting concerned. She hadn't called, and she was not in her hotel room. This doesn't make any sense. She's been out all night. Maybe he scared her. He shouldn't have told her about his crazy life. This doesn't make any sense. Maybe something has happened to her. He'll wait. She'll call.

She didn't call. A day went by. She had checked out of the hotel. Max let a few more days go by before he called the opera company in Canada. He was told that the tour had ended, and everybody had gone home. He called her apartment. She wasn't there. Max had thought that they were closer. At least she could call and say that she had met somebody. He felt she owed him that. Something didn't make sense, but there was nothing he could do. If she changed her feelings, then she changed her feelings. A month went by, and he still heard nothing from her. Theater was like that, great passion, but the curtain also comes down. But something didn't make sense.

CHAPTER 3

Max goes barreling on, this time the construction business. A dear friend of his, named Sophie, married an up-and -coming artist. And boy, did he up and come. No pun, etc. This guy became very famous. He became so famous that he could afford to change from a nice guy to an invention of himself that left something to be desired, at least by Sophie, and in a less important way, by Max. One way to invent one's self is with drugs, but that takes cash, and of course, a particular bend of the mind. This guy had both. But before he rose to great drug-inspired heights, he was really a nice guy who happened to be a kind of a street genius. He had spent a certain time in the can, probably where he learned about the drug option, an option he chose to take.

It was the custom in those days for visual artists who made good to buy a house in the Bowery. Andy Warhol bought a deserted bank, and Sophie's husband bought a little building. Of course, the real estate in that part of town was falling apart. Therefore it was relatively cheap. That was the whole idea. They bought it for nothing and then renovated it. The renovation work was done by the shadow world of workers, draft dodgers, who were keeping their whereabouts close to their chest, a generation of unknown actors, singers, painters, poets, who needed to keep their income sources undiscovered by the Internal Revenue people. They all had a symbiotic place in the lower East Side's food chain. Money was exchanged under the table. Any given Saturday one could observe cops wandering by building sites, chatting with the construction bosses and receiving envelopes, which probably weren't invitations to Bar Mitzvah parties. Building permits weren't in fashion in that part of town. And our boy, Max, was right there among the guys eating fabulous hoagie sandwiches on their lunch break in the Bowery.

Max and a guy named Charles were the president and vice president of the Let's Renovate This Building Inc. They were pooling their knowledge about construction work in an effort to fix up the small building for the famous artist. First you had to gut the building, which wasn't an intellectual challenge. Then you had to familiarize yourself with sheet rock, which actually did require skill, but, hey, Max and Charlie could build rocket ships if given enough time and screwdrivers. Bricklaying was hired out to Italian families. A person can't be expected to know everything. Everything went along smoothly until they cut away half of a floor to make a floor-through. The artist needs space for large paintings. How was Max to know it was a supporting beam? Well, live and learn. As I mentioned, the famous painter was a nice guy in those early days. Adjustments were made, and the renovation continued.

Max's morning walks to the work site were kind of existential, that is, they were about existing. A lot of the morning walks were done in the winter, rainy fucking cold wet winter. He was living with a redhead named Suzan at that time. She was a lovely woman with a slightly crooked nose and the kind of body that was really great to snuggle up with after a hard day on the building site. She made great dinners and the favorite drink was a rosé wine. Breakfast was pork chops, eggs and potatoes, then off to work, stepping over bums who were existing on cardboard placed at the corners of rotting buildings that hadn't been bought yet by famous artists. These bums were, I guess the clinical term is, alcoholics. They are lying around on the sidewalks or walking around in a daze or even joking around, depending on when they had had their last drink. Max stepped over them on his way to work every morning. They came from all over the world. It was a United Nations meeting. They had all gathered to discuss the human condition. Max walks by a lounging bum. He had the feeling he was in the guy's bedroom, invading the guy's private bedroom.

Max mumbles,

"Excuse me."

The bum looks up from his blurry rest, and mutters,

"Got a dollar for a cup of coffee?"

"Sure."

Max gives the guy a dollar. The bum takes the dollar with a kind of élan, his swollen hand receiving its rightful monthly allowance. The bum has a head of sandy hair, thick, like he had cared for it in some other life. The bum smiles at Max like Max was a tourist visiting Alcohol Land. Max had an urge to sit down next to the guy and discuss life as seen from the sidewalk, but he didn't. Max walked on, aware of the bitter weather which the bum seemed to be oblivious to. Max starts talking to himself, mumbling justifications which he felt obliged to come up with.

"This guy's on a short winter vacation. When the vacation's over, he'll die. Why doesn't he straighten things out, get his life together?"
The bum answers him in his mind.

"My life is together as much as yours is."

"I'm not like you. I don't drug myself into oblivion to escape reality."

"Objection! You are just using a different drug. You panhandle for money just like we do. You're a 'success user', an 'image addict'. You don't have any more control over your life than we do. We're all in God's circus, pal, all sitting on the same sidewalk, all swapping sex magazines and knocking back our different versions of Night Train. The sidewalk is time, and yours will run out just like ours will. So have a drink or buy a Mercedes, whichever. Here's looking at you, sweetheart."

Max stumbled on to his quasi-legitimate job. The Bowery population seemed to be looking at Max with glassy triumph. Cold wind and dirt mocked the softie who probably wouldn't last twenty-four hours in this environment. The fact is that Max had admiration for these people. There was something about them that didn't compromise any more. Max got to the work site. Charlie was wiring some lights.

"Hey, Charlie, what do you think about the bums lying around all over the place around here?"

"What do you think about handing me the screwdriver?"

"Come on, what do you think about them?"

"I don't think about it, Max. Fuck 'em. It's not my problem."

Charlie was a blond, curly-headed guy whose green eyes always seemed to look in one direction. He was definitely going somewhere. His life was long and not too wide. Max was always looking around. His visual width slowed him down.

"Give me the fucking screwdriver, Max, and forget the bums. We got to finish early today. I got to get home and clean up. Remember that blonde that came by last week, the one with the great ass? I'm gonna see her later."

The alcoholic lawyer made sense in some nihilistic way. He was right. We can all become addicted to something.

Chrystal slowly began to come to terms with her situation. Of course, she had to leave the tour. It was almost over anyway. She didn't tell the company the full story; only that she had been beaten and robbed. Everybody came to visit her at the hospital before dispersing to his or her various homes spread across the continent. She appreciated their kindness, but she didn't really feel sad that the tour was over. She didn't really feel anything. She knew she should call Max, but something stopped her. She would have to tell him what happened, or make up some reason why she hadn't called. She just didn't want to get into the whole horrible experience again, and the idea of making up a lie made her sick, so she just let the whole thing slide. She would tell him when she saw him again, if she saw him again. She stayed in the hospital a few days. They took the bandage off her face, and she had bruises under her eyes.

When she got back to New York, she moved out of her apartment to a place in the Village. She didn't contact her friends for the same reason she didn't contact Max. She just needed some time. She worked as a temp secretary and tried to figure out what to do with the rest of her life. At times she wished the bastard had killed her, because in a way he had. She didn't feel like singing, and the idea of having a relationship turned her stomach. Time heals all. But what if it doesn't?

Max's life was as chaotic as ever. He had a talent for finding chaos. He thought he would get out of the City for a while, get up to the mountains, but even in the stillness of the Adirondack Mountains, he found a gangster. He had rented a cabin near North Creek, a sleepy mountain town about four hours north of New York City. When he first got there, he looked around at all those woods and regretted his decision to get out of New York City, even for a couple of weeks. OK, books, fishing, fresh air, yeah, yeah, yeah, boring. After a few days he felt better with the quiet. Hiking around, fishing a trout stream, the whole mountain thing became exciting. He began to understand hermits and Native Americans. There was something spectacular about space filled with trees. Not like in a park, more like an ocean of trees and animals. Wild trout meat was pink. Roasted over a fire with corn, it was fabulous. There were absolutely no people around. For miles and miles, no people. Being a tree was normal; maybe he was a kind of a tree, a moving tree. He made noises, and so did the trees. There was a time when trees outnumbered people millions to one. Rocks too. He began talking to the trees and rocks, both silently and out loud. Crazy hermits did that, and he began to understand why, not out of loneliness, but because the trees and rocks were actually saying things, things like, "You are part of us and we are part of you, and we are both part of something else, something unending."

He took to climbing to the top of the surrounding mountains and walking along the crest of one mountain to the next. Then he became part of the sky and the earth and was also air. He was willing to spend the rest of his life in these mountains. Shoot a bear for meat in winter, fish, grow a few vegetables; a person could live here all year. He decided to stay a while longer.

He even tried chewing tobacco. The hectic life of the ambitious city folk suddenly struck him as desperate. He was learning to be patient with himself. 'Let the mountain come to me' was his brave new take on things. Of course, the question was, would a mountain come? This plunge into country life had an element of experiment, an element of the restless wanderer going through his bag of questions, his bag of freedoms.

"Where is this road going to take me?"

He began to write. He felt that truth would come to him if he were sitting down, so he sat down and wrote. He had spent the early part of his life in a volcano breathing sulfur, so his first stories were about young burning, lots of women and weird characters, but also about a childhood in Tennessee, a childhood with strange, recovering parents. The stories were naive. They had the smell of virgin sweat. He wanted to get his thoughts down so he would know, but then he was sick of knowing and didn't want to know. He wanted to not know. He craved questions which had no answer, because he felt that having no answer *was* the answer. What was the miracle of birth or the explanation of splendor? Riding the waves of mystery was thrilling, stories in bed with poetry.

It was while Max was in the mountains that he got a call from his father. Max had left his mountain number on his answering machine in the City. Max hadn't had much contact with his parents since he took off one summer when he was about fifteen and went to Florida. He had called a few times when he had been at the University of North Carolina, but only a few times. He had received a scholarship to the University, so he was financially independent and emotionally independent more or less as well. He had phoned a few times, as students do, to say hello. Kids always call their parents when they are away to say how great everything is, to sound adult and independent and hear that they are missed and loved. Max's father had even surprised him with a visit to the university. They ate lunch together in the school cafeteria, then Max's father drove away after the lunch together, but that was several years ago, several years before this call to the mountains.

     "Hello, Max. It's your father. How are you?"

     "Fine, Dad. How's Mom?"

     "Mom's in the hospital, son."

"What's the matter with her?"

"She tried to commit suicide. She's been in a lot of pain because of her back. She's had a lot of trouble with her back."

"Is she OK?"

"She's OK."

"Do you want me to come there? I'll catch a plane."

"I'll arrange the ticket."

Max got a ride out of the mountains and flew to Chattanooga, Tennessee. His father met him at the airport.

The airport at Chattanooga is a small airport with a proud display of the first Coca Cola bottles. The Coca Cola industry had started near Chattanooga. Max's father was soft and worried when he picked Max up, and they drove to the hospital. Max's mother was lying in some sheets on the small hospital bed. She didn't react very much to Max.

"How are you feeling, Mom?"

She still didn't react. Maybe she was sleeping. She had taken a lot of sleeping pills. Max's father couldn't wake her the morning after she had taken the pills, and he found a note next to the bed. It said 'I'm sorry'. Max's father called an ambulance which immediately brought her to the hospital.

"How are you feeling, Mom?"

"You don't know pain, son."

Then she dozed off again. Max held on to the aluminum bar that was at the side of the bed. He watched his mother for a while. Then he and his father went to the hospital cafeteria and had a cup of coffee.

Max stayed a few days in Chattanooga. He slept in his old bed. His mother got better. She would begin to get psychiatric help. Max's father drove him back to the airport, and they were close and kissed each other on the side of the face, then Max flew back to the mountains.

It had turned cold in North Creek. One day something went wrong with the plumbing in his cabin. Maybe a water pipe had frozen up. He took a walk along the asphalt road near his cabin. About a mile down the asphalt road there was a rocky dirt road that must lead to somewhere. He followed it. He came to a small hotel in the middle of nowhere. The hotel consisted of a main house made of grey stone with twenty or thirty hotel rooms and a small building next to it. No one was around, no one in the main house, no one in the small building next to it. What the hell was this hotel doing here? There was no sign advertising the hotel. Maybe it wasn't a hotel. What the hell was it? Fifty yards or so from this construction, whatever it was, was a normal-looking home. Maybe they would know something. Max goes over and knocks on the door. A man comes to the door. He looks at first to be a teenager, but then he seems older, maybe about forty, burr haircut like a teenager, but the physical build of a powerful wrestler. His neck is almost as wide as his shoulders.

"Can I help you?"

"Yes, hello, I'm staying in a cabin up the road, and the plumbing is out of order. Is there a plumber around here somewhere?"

"I'll take a look at it. I'll get some tools."

Three young kids come to the door, two girls and a boy and a dark-headed woman.

"This here is my wife and my kids. I'm Harry. This is Suzy and Judy, and this here is Henry, and my wife Nancy."

Harry goes to get his tools.

"Thanks a lot. I'm Max. Don't mean to trouble you."

Nancy's voice is simple and honest-sounding,

"It'll be no trouble. Harry's just taking it easy. You want some coffee?"

"No thanks. Say, who runs that hotel over there?"

Harry returns with his toolbox.

"We run it. It belongs to my boss."

"Was just curious, does it do much business?"

"Not much," Harry says, "Just for special guests."

Max has been around long enough to know when to quit asking questions.

Max and Harry go down the road to the cabin, and Harry fixes the water pipes. I guess Harry does a lot of things. He talks about a book he is writing for children, about a tribe of people who live in a burned-out volcano near the center of the earth. He also has another project going, carving wooden Indians for local tobacco stores. He is a bubbly person, even younger than a teenager, giving no hint whatsoever about a certain aspect of his personality Max would later discover. Harry fixes the problem and when Max asks,

"How much do I owe you?"

"Nothing, come on over for a drink anytime you want. The hotel has a great bar and a great restaurant."

Well, this is too much for Max to resist. Nature is great, but what the hell is going on around here. The next evening Max shows up at the grey stone 'hotel'. Harry and some men are sitting at a beautiful bar made out of dark wood. Harry is happy to see Max and introduces him to the three men who are definitely not from North Creek. They are dressed in Little Italy Casual. Harry invites Max to a dinner of pasta and scallops. Harry has a special thing for scallops. After dinner the men sit in front of a fireplace made of granite. It seems that granite is plentiful in the area. The fireplace is huge, a walk-in fireplace, big enough to roast a cow in. Max explains that he is an actor, which seems to please the Little Italy contingent. He tells a few jokes, which Max is good at, and the evening is sparkling along. Slowly the picture begins to become clearer, as clear as these kind of pictures get. The hotel is a tax write-off and a money-laundering device. The boss, whoever that is, is involved in different enterprises, all of which don't exist, and Harry is in charge of this one. It's a cushy job. Harry is also a melter.

A melter is someone who melts silver coins illegally. In the fifties, dimes, quarters etc. were made of silver. The deal was you melt, say, a thousand dollars worth of dimes into a bar of silver. Well, silver as bar is worth, say, five thousand dollars. Of course, there are several crimes involved in this process. One is how the dimes were obtained in the first place. And, of course, this was just an example. They didn't deal in thousand dollar amounts, they dealt in million dollar amounts.

When involved in this kind of business, you needed friends with certain capabilities. Aside from skills in theft and knowledge of metallurgy, one had to have a reputation as a person one didn't want to offend. Harry, it turns out, when angry, broke people's knees. In fact, if you got on the wrong side of Harry, the only sensible thing to do was to leave the state for a year or two, until Harry cooled down.

It was the little things that made Harry upset. Hearts, for instance. Hearts is a card game, not the most exciting game in the world, but Harry loved to play it. You didn't have to let Harry win. He was a good loser. It's just that when Harry wanted to play—best not to say no. Refusing to play Hearts upset Harry. It insulted his dignity. You could spend the rest of your life limping for a thing like that.

The other side of the medallion is that Harry would give his right arm for someone he cared for. Max got into some difficulty once with a guy who sold bus tickets. Max had been visiting Harry and the mountains. The guy sold Max the wrong return ticket back to New York and wouldn't give him his money back. An altercation ensued, causing minor damage to the office. The ticket salesman called the police, and Max called Harry. Harry got there first. He entered the premises, stepping over some broken things and went over to the complainant and asked,

"What's the trouble?"

The complainant looked up into Harry's inquiring face and said, wisely,

"No trouble."

Max and Harry left the premises, and Harry drove Max back to New York, calming him down all the while by telling him the children's story about the little people who lived in the volcano.

Max's time in the mountains came to an end. He had to get back to the sidewalks, make some money, see some women friends. Maybe Suzan was around. He could write in the city. He wrote about his life as a young American Jew with one foot in an unlimited future and one foot in a tragic past.

There was this viaduct at the top of a hill on East 5th Street in Chattanooga, Tennessee. Max's mother and father started their life in the United States down the street from this viaduct. There was a synagogue within walking distance from the house, not that Mr. and Mrs. Fagan were religious. No one was religious after the war. You ate everything, kosher or not, and you were glad to get it. Mr. and Mrs. Fagan actually got fat, partly because they were getting older, and partly because they ate trying to erase not eating. The thing about the viaduct was that it was strange, this huge concrete wall at the top of the hill. It was about fifteen feet tall, which made climbing on it dangerous, and also it stopped cars. When the cars came up the street and reached the viaduct, they had to turn right or left. Max always thought it looked like a pyramid, a piece of Egypt in the neighborhood. It was a strange huge thing.

Max went to school in Chattanooga, Tennessee, regular school, then after regular school he went to this Hebrew school, which was next to the synagogue. The Hebrew school had these huge black Hebrew letters on posters tacked to the walls. Max came to the Hebrew school after regular school and played softball with his Hebrew classmates while waiting for class to start. The young students came into the classroom covered with dust from the softball field. Usually the sun was just about to set at this time, the sunlight coming through the windows and making the black religious books along the walls look majestic and holy, which they were anyway.

Max's parents had two rules. The deal was that he wasn't supposed to have girlfriends who weren't Jewish, or to climb on the viaduct. Of course he did both, and both were dangerous. He had more bruises from the non-Jewish thing than from falling off the viaduct. That was the weird thing about Max's youth. One minute there was this happy home thing, and another minute there was getting beat all to hell with the buckle of his belt. Things set it off like disobeying the girlfriend rule or like leaving schoolbooks on the kitchen table. Max's mother was the stranger of the two parents, and she had these wide open eyes, wider than they should have been. There was enough light around. Her eyes were just very open, like with frozen fear. Max's father was soft and worried.

Wenonah was the dangerous one. That's a Native American name. She was the one that got Max into a lot of trouble. He had a lot of stripes on his back with her name on them. They met after school and did the walk. When they got out of sight from the school guys, they found a place to kiss, and she let Max feel her young breasts. She felt around plenty too.

Max came home one afternoon 'late'. He put his schoolbooks on the kitchen table. That's two out of two. His mother's wide eyes were very wide.

"Why you put the books on the table?" Slap.

"I told you, the books belong in your room." Slap.

"Why you so late from school?"

Max was about twelve, and he had developed some pretty good defense reflexes over the years, which came in handy when he was older and did a little boxing. Anyway, his mother went for the belt. She tried to take it off Max, but Max had gotten strong enough to hold on to it. The being hit phase of his life was over. Maybe his mother finally saw the cruelty of her ways, or maybe she was just getting tired. There was a black eye incident a few years later, but the main beating phase had come to an end.

The next day, Max and Wenonah were doing the forbidden, and Max told her about the latest episode.

"Why doesn't your father stop her?"

"Dad doesn't know about it."

"Well, tell him, Max. Tell him. He'll tell her to quit hitting you."

"I'm taking off in a few years, when I'm a little older. I'm going to Florida. Live on the beach. You want to come with me?"

They had their special place, Max and Wenonah. It was under some wooden stairs on the back of an old grey house.

"You want to come with me, Wenonah?"

She let Max put his hand on her nipples, then under her panties. He loved to feel the miracle of fuzz that was starting to come between her young legs.

"I'll come with you, Max."

They kissed and enjoyed the late afternoon together.

There was another side to the story with Max's parents, another side that was also part of the stories he wrote, the part about the days when his parents were young and lived at 142 Boulevard de l'Hôpital in Paris. The stories came out after a meal, after a schnaps. His father had worked on the open market, sold underwear, socks, that sort of thing. Up at five, cognac and coffee, load the car and drive to a village near Paris and set up shop on the open market. "Madame, demandez les prix, toujours les prix!" He called in a loud hoarse voice that the women should ask the price, always ask the price. Max's mother's wide eyes gripped Max.

"Your aunt and uncle and cousin lived a few doors down the street. When the Nazis occupied Paris, that's a funny thing to say, occupied Paris, maybe raped Paris, anyway, when they were there in Paris, they took your uncle Michel and your aunt Fanny and little Luc."

She stopped, and then went on.

"I mean, they would have been your uncle and aunt and cousin."

She stopped again.

"The Nazis took them out of their apartment and put them in a truck. The conçierge had informed the police and whoever handled the Jewish information. Papa and I left Paris and went to the country and hid. We were taken in by a farm family, a Christian farm family by the name of

Granjean, Monsieur and Madame Grandjean and two little children, Jacques and Mireille. The family gave us crosses to wear, crosses on a gold chain. We worked as hired hands on the farm, Christian hired hands."

Max's mother took a sip of schnaps.

"German soldiers would come by every now and then and ask to see everybody's papers. 'Ausweis bitte'. We didn't have any Ausweis papers, so we hid when we saw them coming. We hid until the soldiers putted away on their motorcycle and sidecar. One afternoon the soldiers came by at lunch time, and we didn't have time to run to our hiding-place. The soldiers were polite, always polite. The Grandjeans asked them if they would like to join them for lunch. The soldiers politely refused and asked to see the papers."

As Max's mother told the story, her eyes returned to normal size. Max's father drank schnaps and looked at nothing in front of him. Max heard all this with a mixture of pain and guilt that he hadn't been there to be a superman and save them, and pride that such brave people were his parents.

"So the soldiers asked for the papers and the one who was in charge, the one who always sat in the sidecar, saw that we didn't have papers. He saw that we were Jews. The soldier looked into my face and saw that I was Jewish and terrified, and the officer smiled and thanked the Grandjeans for the invitation and left. They putted away like clowns in a black and white Charlie Chaplin movie. Two days later a truck came, and we were all forced to get into the truck. The Grandjean children didn't cry. They thought it was a great adventure that they had begun, an adventure ride. We got in the truck and were driven to the train station in the village. We, papa and I, were told to get out and join a group of people who were waiting for a train. The Grandjeans were told to stay in the truck which drove away. We never saw the Grandjeans again. We kept the crosses until they were later taken away from us."

These memories were the things Max wrote about up in the mountains and then later in the City. The whole idea was to throw away everything that was in his mind, just unload it all into stories so he could get to the beach, the clean beach, the clean sea air with a little fish smell and fermenting life smell, just break free, like he did when he was about fifteen, like he told Wenonah he would.

When he was fifteen, he 'hit the road Jack' and slept along the way here and there, more or less like he was doing now in the City. He had no idea of who he really was or where he was really going. He didn't have the luxury of being on the edge of existence, where the philosophical issue, at least, was clear. No Cossacks were after him, no Nazis. He didn't come to New York with the 'huddled masses yearning to be free'. He came to burn carbon. To find the diamond. Sure, there was room in this city for his furnace. He could burn through women and colorful characters until the cows came home, but what was the point? Was he getting closer to his diamond, or was he, like many New York aspiring hopefuls, at the end of the journey and just didn't know it? The train had pulled out, and he would join the stranded. Max was scared. He had had his moments on the stage, but so what? Maybe the answer was to thumb across the country. Get away from the stage drug. Go over the mountain, have the guts to join the real restless. Just drift. You're a drifter, Max. Admit it and accept it. Otherwise, you have to play the game. Make the rounds. Get an agent. Get a photo. Go to parties. Catch the fish in mid-air and bow to the Circus Master.

CHAPTER 4

Max kept on writing and thinking about the lawyer bum in his imaginary conversation in the Bowery. Was he an addict, like the bum said, 'success addicted'? Did he need the 'approval fix' from the trainer? Was he a dancing bear with a collar around his neck, a collar stained with sweat and inlaid with fake jewels? Maybe he was one of God's clowns in search of his own circus. He felt as if his life was being controlled by a series of robots, every one telling him what he should be doing, what he should be thinking, grading his life performance. Unpredictable mirth was out. It was naïve to think in simple terms. Chrystal thought in simple terms, at least Max thought so. It turned out that she was not so simple. Dark intellect weighed with self-observation; weight which made sudden flights into quicksilver-truth impossible. For many, Disneyland was the extreme state of well-being. In a word, hopelessness was chic.

The antidote to this situation was Shakespeare. Max liked Shakespeare. Along with all those round vowels, there was a room full of open doors in Shakespeare's plays, a room full of choices. You were free to be simple or complicated or both. You could be the clown playing to the children of any age, and then plunge into profound murky thoughts, then spin around on a poetic merry-go-round and slide into freedom, and that's more or less what Max did. In other words, he ran into Chrystal.

The Shakespeare Festival was having auditions. Max hadn't seen her for over a year, and suddenly there she was, as dark and vulnerable as always, perhaps even more so. The auditions took place down near Cooper Union. The actors and actresses were in a room waiting to be called. Chrystal was standing near a window but looking more into herself than out of the window. She had decided to try the stage again, not as a singer, as an actress. Max enjoyed looking at her from the perspective of his knowing that she was there, but she not knowing that he was there. Quietly he came up behind her and whispered, "Hello."
She spun around. The face, which had been filled with quiet thought, was now filled with terror.
        "Oh!"
        "Chrystal, it's Max. I'm sorry. I didn't mean to scare you."
He gently held her shoulders. Her body became a piece of steel. She pushed him away.
        "Chrystal, it's me, Max. Are you OK?"
        "Max!"
She threw her arms around him as if he had just saved her from falling off a cliff. She began to tremble.
        "Chrystal, easy, it's OK."
He held her until she became calm.
        "I'm sorry, Max. I'm OK."
Suddenly she was all right.
        "Max! How the hell are you?"
        "I'm fine. How are you?"

"Let's get the hell out of here. I owe you a drink."

"Who scared who the most?"

"I scared you more than you scared me."

"No. Me more."

"No. Me more."

They were back in step.

They went to a coffee shop in the Village. Max didn't ask questions. He figured that if she had something to say, she would say it. If not, then not.

Chrystal was living on Bank Street. She looked different to Max. Her innerness was even more so. She still exploded her feelings like she always did, but the expansion had something guarded about it. Something was over her shoulder, something dark. And there was something else, her face was scarred.

"Did you get a face lift?"

It was meant as a joke, but as soon as he said it, he knew it wasn't funny.

"I had an accident, bicycle accident."

"Looks great. I could use a bicycle accident."

"Sandy opened an exercise place, up on 73rd. I haven't seen any of the old cast. Have you?"

"No. Sandy went to Europe for a while to get her opera career going. I guess she didn't like Germany. She came back and got this health studio going. Hey, what can I tell you? That's how the noodles cook. So you didn't marry and settle down?"

"Who would want to marry me? You want to marry me?"

"Let's finish the coffee first."

"I don't need men in my life. I live alone, and that's fine."

"Did you become a lesbian?"

"No, but it's an idea."

"You know what Woody Allen said, 'Don't forget lesbian sex, that's my favorite kind.' So what's with you and men? Did you have a bad time with some guy? You can shut me up if I get too nosy."

"No, I haven't been in a relationship for a while now, been busy. I've got to head uptown. Doctor's appointment."

"I got the coffee, even though you scared me the most. I'd like to see you. You got a phone?"

"Here's my number. I'm a little late."

She gets up and starts out of the coffee shop. Max stands up, a little confused. She goes out the door. Max stands there, puzzled. Suddenly she runs back into the coffee shop. She kisses Max on the lips.

"I'd like to see you too."

Chrystal looks at Max's face. She wants to say many things. She says nothing and runs out the door. Max pays the bill and walks out onto the street. Chrystal is in trouble. He looks at the phone number in his hand. This whole thing had never made sense, and it still didn't. He had forgotten all about the audition. It was too late now anyway. What the hell is going on with Chrystal? He remembered her openness, her warmth. He remembered what he thought was love. He gets the IRT uptown.

Later that night, he stared out his living room window at the White Hall Hotel. The backside of the hotel faced the backside of his building. It was a welfare hotel. The city owned it, and it provided shelter for the homeless. God knows what went on in that hotel. Occasionally an empty whiskey bottle came flying out of a window. Max expected a person to come flying out any minute. A building filled with desperate people. Was he right in thinking Chrystal was desperate, or was the White Hall Hotel mucking up Max's mind? What had happened in Chicago? It was only eight. He'd give her a call. Damned answering machine. He left a message.

Bicycle accident? He felt like he was responsible for her well-being somehow, which was ridiculous. She had left *him*, so to speak. She wasn't in an opera he was directing, or a play. He didn't like to play the father-protector with women. He loved her. It was that simple. Seeing her opened up a road for him. He could either go down that road or stand still, which is what he had been doing his whole life. Where the hell was she anyway? Bank Street, where on Bank Street?

About three in the morning, Max's telephone rang. Max's head was full of bourbon and sleep. It had to ring several times.

"Hello."

"It's Chrystal."

"Who?"

"I'm sorry to wake you up. Go back to sleep."

"Chrystal?"

"I'm sorry, Max. Go back to sleep."

"Chrystal? Is that you?"

"It's me, Max."

"Chrystal, for Christ's sake. I love you."

There is a long pause.

"I love you too."

"Where are you?"

"I'm home."

"Well, where the hell is home?"

"Bank Street. 148 Bank Street."

"I'll be there as soon as I can get there. What time is it?"

"It's around three."

"Are you all right?"

"Maybe tomorrow would be better."

"I'll see you in about thirty minutes."

"OK."

Max caught a cab. She buzzed him in. Max looked into Chrystal's grey face. Slowly her face began to crumble. She began gasping, crying, her chest heaving. She tried to speak between gasps.

"Max... I've... been... raped!"

"What? When? Tonight? Easy, darling, easy. Tell me. What happened?"

"Not tonight. Last year... while I was on tour... in Chicago."

Max held her. They swayed gently.

"Tell me darling. Tell me."

"That's why I had to leave so quickly... I'm seeing a therapist... I saw her yesterday. Thursdays... I see her Thursdays... Max I can't ... I can't love... I mean... sex... I have to tell you. Don't love me... It won't work. I had to tell you. I saw how you looked at me... how I looked back. I've been wanting to tell you for so long. But it won't work. Now you know, so just go, and please stay my friend. I need your friendship more than anything in the world."

"I didn't come here to make love, I came to love. If you want, you can tell me about it, if not, we can just talk about old times. Remember crazy Sandy and her mysterious sugar daddy? Sit down. You got some coffee? I love you, Chrystal. No one will hurt you."

For a long time, they didn't talk. They just sat. Morning came. Max had dozed off. Chrystal sat staring out the window.

They spent the next days and nights together. Slowly Chrystal opened. It was not the rape, the shame, the humiliation that was freezing her, it was the anger. She wanted to kill him. There was a man, she wanted to kill him and she couldn't. The police couldn't find him. Even if they did... her therapist told her she had to talk about it, get it out. Max asked for details. She explained it was after a performance. It was around twelve, midnight. She had hurried back to the hotel, intending to phone Max. But as she opened her door to her room, a man came at her from behind, pushed her onto the floor. He beat her face violently, and she passed out. When she came to, she was alone, half-naked and bleeding. She managed to call the reception and told them she'd been raped. She was in a hospital about three days. Then she came back to New York. When she got back, she had some problems sleeping, and she couldn't concentrate on anything. Her mind wandered. She would be doing something, and suddenly she would forget what she was doing. She got some help from a therapist, but she didn't see a great future for herself.

Max listened. A question came up in his mind. He didn't ask it, he just noticed it. If Chrystal could kill this bastard or have him killed, would she be freed from her psychological problem? This unasked question had several aspects. Was the solution morally acceptable? Was it possible? Should he put the question to her? And where was Harry? Harry had disappeared from the 'hotel' in the mountains. Max had tried to get in touch with him on several occasions, but he had left. Maybe if Chrystal thought she had the option, then that might make her feel better. If he could find Harry, find out if Harry knew how to get the information, and, if yes, just give her the choice, would that loosen the knot around her heart? This scum is dangerous to the general population. Of course, the legal route is the preferable route. Let the police bring this criminal to justice. But when the police ask around, nobody knows nothing. When Harry's acquaintances pose questions, answers come pouring forth, or something else comes pouring forth. Besides, this kind of crime is not well looked upon by the underworld community. Just questions kicking around in Max's mind.

Several months passed. Max quit trying to understand the world's problems and concentrated on trying to solve Chrystal's problem. He spent as much time with her as he could. Chrystal went through periods when things looked like they might straighten out. Then suddenly she would freeze, go away. She was a woman with enormous energy and passion. In a way, that was the problem. When her inner volcanoes exploded, everything was all right, when they imploded, she burned her guts out.

They were lying next to each other one afternoon. They were one and not one. Neither could leave, and staying was a pain that they shared because they needed to share something. Chrystal was staring into herself. Max gently touched her face.

"You could shoot him."

Chrystal turned toward Max, her eyes slowly focused. Max thought she was angry with him. He felt sick and stupid. He had hurt her. She glared at him. He had never seen her glare at him. The oneness they had shared was destroyed. He had ruined it. She spoke very gently.

" I would love that."

It sounded as if Max had suggested some sexual fantasy, and she had agreed to it. The glare turned to a kiss. Her teeth bit his lip. Her tongue fought through his surprised mouth. Rape energy poured from her into his body then back from him, back into hers. It was strange. Perverse. Wonderful.

Chrystal needed the option. The question was how to deal with this bastard. One thing was sure. Chrystal wanted him dead. The next question, where was Harry? Slowly the situation was taking shape. Chrystal became more like herself. They had pummeled into a new dimension, a Shakespearian dimension. Justice could become a real possibility. They had agreed to enter a domain they both needed to enter, a forbidden domain. Like passion was a forbidden domain, killing was a forbidden domain. They had found their circus.

Where was Harry? Harry had mentioned a small town in Alabama, Sweetwater. Sure nuff, he found Harry Sims—that was his last name—with address and phone number. Max calls the number. No answer. An hour later Max gets a call.

"Max?"

"Harry! Great to hear your voice! How ya doin'?"

"Fine. Know any new jokes?"

"Where are you? There's something I want to ask you."

"I'm in the City on Thursday. Wanna have lunch?"

"Great, Harry. You still like hamburgers? There's a great hamburger place on Broadway and about 84th, Big Nick's. Is that OK?"

"See you around 1:00."

Click.

Harry didn't like to talk much on the phone.

Max and Harry met at Big Nick's. They took a booth in the back. They didn't talk about the situation until later. They took a walk in Central Park, and Max told Harry what he knew, what Chrystal had told him. Harry wanted to know some details, what the guy looked like and where it happened.

"I don't know the name of the hotel, the one near the theatre where she was performing."

"Does she remember what he looked like?"

"I don't think she will ever forget what he looked like."

"So what you got in mind if I can find out anything?"

"I don't know. It's mainly Chrystal's decision."

"Goddamned bastard ought to have his balls cut off."

"Is there a way I can get in touch with you?"

"I'll give you a call. Give me a couple weeks."

"Harry, what do I owe you?"

"Tell me the joke about the Rabbi and the prostitute."

Max told him the joke.

Chrystal and Max more or less moved in together. They kept their separate apartments but stayed mainly at Max's. It was a little larger than hers. It wasn't like a miracle happened and she was suddenly a happy person. It was more like her life had a piece added to it, a piece she wanted to hold on to, a piece of freedom. She didn't tell her therapist about what she had in mind. She did mention that her sex life was great, but she didn't go into detail. They went about their lives and waited to hear from Harry.

It was an interesting wait, not like you're waiting to hear about a part in a play, or to find out if you passed a test. Questions kept coming up, like how do you actually do it, shoot someone? Do you say 'Hey asshole, remember me?' and then shoot him in the chest? It has to be quick. Bang Bang. What if you miss? What kind of weapon do you use? Where the hell do you get a gun? Would Harry really be able to find out anything? This happened in Chicago. Does he actually know anybody in Chicago? Max hadn't discussed with Harry *who* would do it. Maybe Harry thought he was to arrange for someone in Chicago to do it. That would sort of miss the point.

Max got a call from Harry. They met at Big Nick's. Then they took a walk in the park. Harry told Max what he found out.

"A guy, a certain Roger Jones, has a rep for this kind of shit, mainly young women, did some time for rape, real low life. He does his shit then brags about it. I got a copy of his record. There's a photo. If your friend says this is the right guy, for 1,000 dollars she can have whatever she wants done."

"Harry, what do I owe you?"

"Tell me the joke about the kid from the Mafia boss."

Max told him the joke.

Max knew that having the guy bumped off would bring no closure for Chrystal. She wanted to pull the trigger herself. There was the question of the gun. What kind of gun? Was 'gun' even the correct terminology? Buying a weapon was a complicated project. You have to get clearance for a license. Harry would know what to do, but they couldn't make Harry do everything. What about Max's old friend, Jose? This seemed right up Jose's alley. Max takes a trip to Harlem.

It had been over a year since Max had seen Jose. The Oasis was still there, but where the hell would Jose be? Max didn't feel comfortable waltzing into the Oasis and asking questions. Nobody would answer the questions anyway. Jose was not at his old guard post. The game had probably moved a thousand times in the past year.

There was this guy Thomas. Thomas was a chess player. An island separated the uptown avenue from the downtown avenue. There were benches on this island and a little grass and a concrete chess table. Thomas had learned to play chess in prison, and he got pretty good at it. One could find Thomas sitting at this chess table in all kinds of weather, day or night. He was a good friend of Jose's. Max left word with Thomas that he would be there tomorrow about this time.

It was good to see Jose. He hadn't changed. He hadn't even changed clothes. They went to the soul food place, Max's treat. Jose was curious.

"What the hell you need a gun for?"

"It's not for me. Someone I love."

"You getting a gun for a woman? Man, you crazy."

Max told Jose the story. Jose understood.

"You want me to do this? I'll lay the mother fucker flat."

"It's her choice. You got to meet her. Come over for dinner next week. What you doing Wednesday?"

"I'll be there."

Max wrote down the address. It would be a special event. Jose rarely left Harlem.

Jose showed up around eight. Max didn't know who was more nervous, Jose or Chrystal. She fixed Italian food. Pasta, veal cacciatore, wine, the works. Jose didn't know much about Italian food, but he seemed to like it, and he liked Chrystal. All the talk was from the gut. There was no small talk.

"You folks should have some children. A woman wants to have children, Max. You better give her some children."

"We're not married, Jose."

"Dat don't make no difference. If you want to keep her, you'd better get some young'uns. She's a pretty woman, Max. You got a great smile Chrystal, big warm smile. You hear what I'm tellin' you, Max."

Max's face was serious.

"What do you think about that, honey?"

Chrystal smiled, just smiled.

Jose explained some things about the weapon. To begin with, it was a common handgun, a so-called 'Saturday night special', the number removed, no way to find out where it came from.

"Chrystal honey, you sure you can do this? Now my ex-wife, she could do it, but you're different. Why don't you let me take care of this?"

Chrystal joked, "You might get hurt, Jose. I would have a bad conscience if you were to get hurt."

"Here's a box of bullets."

He showed her how to load the weapon.

Max observed the whole encounter between Chrystal and Jose with a kind of distance. He was a part of the team but not a main player, not yet. The whole gun thing was fascinating. This nickel-plated dispenser of death was not so far removed from the cap guns he played with as a child. Chrystal's small gentle white hands holding a silver toy, Jose's older, dark-skinned hands holding a weapon, their handing the mysterious object back and forth, each momentarily pointing at an imaginary victim, their finger around the trigger.

"Jose, we're going to need more bullets, maybe five boxes."

"Five boxes! You gonna start a war?"

"I think she should shoot the gun a few times to practice."

"Five boxes?" Jose looked at Max. "You right, five boxes."

The conversation didn't dwell on Chicago. Jose talked about his children. He didn't have much contact with them, and that obviously was a painful thing in his life. There was no big love loss between him and his ex. A few months ago Jose's son got in touch with him to inform him that Jose's daughter was getting married. He hadn't been invited to the wedding, but he went anyway. The daughter was a WAC in the army. She had met a guy while she was stationed in Germany, a white guy. The reunion had been tearful. He gave the newly-weds some money and got along well with his new son-in-law. "You folks better get some children."

The evening had been more about life than about death.

CHAPTER 5

Chrystal continued working as a temporary secretary. Her jobs varied from week to week, yet they didn't vary, always the same kind of people, just different faces. It was OK, and it was money, but she found it fascinating that her colleagues went home to their normal lives, and she went home to continue planning the death of one Roger Jones. It was interesting that no one who knew about the project questioned her right to do this, no one close to her. Max didn't. Jose didn't. Harry, whoever he is, didn't. Of course, if she brought up a theoretical situation to her friends—does someone have the right to kill someone who raped you?—she would get the usual arguments against killing, against capital punishment, against anarchy, etc. They might make an exception in the case of Hitler or Genghis Kahn. She herself would have been against killing them if she hadn't experienced the rape. Whatever the arguments were, when she came home after work, she took out the files with the picture on them, and she took out her weapon and felt no inner conflict about killing the man in the picture. The main problem was deciding when.

Max rented a car, and they drove to the Adirondacks. Max wanted to show Chrystal the mountains, and they needed a place to go to fire the weapon. They drove to the old cabin Max had rented. Max felt as if it were many years ago. The cabin was empty. It looked like no one had lived in it for a long time. They drove to the hotel where Max had met Harry. The place was all boarded up, no one around. Then they took a long walk, way back in the woods. Max wanted to show Chrystal everything he knew, everything he felt about the woods. He wanted to take her to the top of the mountains where he had walked. He wanted her to feel she was talking to the trees. Chrystal wanted to shoot the gun. They reached a spot where the experiment could take place. Chrystal took the weapon out of her jacket pocket and loaded it.

"Well, here goes."

She straightened her arm and pointed in no particular direction, squinted and pulled the trigger. There was a bang that sounded like a firecracker. The gun had a kick to it, which jerked her hand up. The whole thing startled her, and she started laughing.

"Well, did I get him?"

"Definitely."

They laughed and she tried again. The result was pretty much the same as the first time. Now it was Max's turn. He had seen enough TV to get the right look in the face and more or less the right stance. He fired, and if the victim cooperated and didn't move for a few seconds, he might have been hit. Max had a suggestion.

"Hold the gun in both hands and straighten your arms out in the direction of the bastard you want to hit. Don't aim, just look at him and fire. You won't be that far away. Try that."

This seemed to work better for her. She began to get the feeling. She reloaded. Max continued to advise.

"Play like this tree is the guy. Try that!"
Chrystal got a serious look on her face and went to town on the tree. If it had been a man, it would be a dead man. She emptied the weapon into the tree. She reloaded. She got better and better. Suddenly the glare came into her eyes. She fired again and again. She killed the asshole again and again in her mind, firing accurately and with a cool savage face. She emptied four boxes of ammunition into the tree, smashing the wood and bark into splinters. Suddenly she was exhausted. Her arms dropped. She gasped for breath. Max put his arms around her. She turned to him, her face wet with tears.

"I love you, Max. I love you so… much."

The weapon fell from her hands. She caressed his face. Her twisted mouth found his and they fell to the ground entwined into each other. They undressed each other and rolled into each other, and when they came, the trees spoke.

Max and Harry had one last meeting. Harry gave Max the information he needed: where this bastard lived, what bar he frequented and when the best time to do the job might be. It seemed he took a subway home about midnight most nights. He took the subway near the theatre where Chrystal had performed. That was probably the best opportunity. Harry was concerned about Max's lack of experience in these matters, but Harry had a lot of faith in Max. Max didn't tell Harry that Chrystal would shoot. No need to complicate the issue.

When Chrystal slept, the blood from the tree went into the earth and cried out to her. Her dreams were

71

of trees smashed and torn by the bullets. The trees were not dead but were crippled and in pain. They met Chrystal's glare and asked 'Why us? Why did you shoot one of us?' In her dreams she had to deal with the trees. She dreamed of the snow-covered trees in the Alaskan forests. When she was awake, the problem of feeling for the trees was not a serious problem, but when she slept, the trees had faces and voices and their sap was blood, and the earth on which the lovers had rolled cried out in her dreams. The snow-coated trees of her memories were stained with blood. She talked about it to Max.

"I feel bad about shooting the tree."

"The tree was just for practicing. When you have shot the bastard, the tree will become a tree again."

"What if it doesn't? What if I have lost my right to love trees? I didn't hate the thick trunk. I fired bullets into it, now it is scarred and its skin is removed in places. It didn't see the scum hit me and feel my private body. The tree thinks I hate it. Can we go back to the mountains and talk with it?"

"We will go back into the sea of trees and try to find a bridge to them. You can try to explain the problem about being violated and being raped and beaten up. Maybe the trunk will give you some sort of forgiveness, some sort of feeling that the ripping into its bark isn't such a tragedy."

"What if the blood of this asshole comes after me? His blood isn't him. His blood is just borrowed like the tree's blood, borrowed from some life pool so the tree can live. This scum has borrowed the blood so he can misuse the life juice.

What if the scum's blood gets into my sleep like the tree's blood did?"

"You have a choice, Chrystal. We are where we are. We can't go back as if it didn't happen. You will choose, and we will move on together."

Chrystal spent many hours with her mind in the forest. She liked nature as people do, but this intimate experience, where the trees witnessed her hate and her love, made them a part of her. When she saw them, she saw herself, saw Max and didn't see the scum she had seen in her fury. She saw someone she had harmed. The trees swayed above her asking 'Why?' They didn't accuse her. They just wondered why it was important for her to break their surface, tear their container of life.

"Can we go to the mountains again soon?"

"What about Chicago? Maybe we should get this behind us before the New Year."

"There is an order, Max. Important things have an order. We are more the trees than we are the project. When we have made peace, then we will do the project."

Chrystal began to feel guilty because she couldn't make a clear decision. Before the afternoon in the trees she had been very clear. Life was very clear. But what she did in the woods was wrong. She was wrong. Why hadn't she been more careful that night? Why hadn't she sensed danger? This whole thing was beginning to be her fault. Now she had brought Max into the picture, and all Max's friends. She was always being too friendly with strangers. All her life she was too open, too friendly. Why didn't she use her head, damn it!

"Chrystal, you are getting angry with the wrong person. Why? Why? Why are you the guilty one all of the sudden?"

"I have to accept my part in this mess. I can't just say, 'Hey, I'm innocent, the rest of the world is guilty'. That's what's wrong with the world today. Nobody takes the blame for their own part in the world's mess."

"Fuck the world, Chrystal. This has nothing to do with the world. It just happened *in* the world."

"I'm just as guilty as the bastard was. What if it was his body instead of the tree trunk's? I'm capable of violence, just as he is. I enjoyed killing him. Did you notice that? Did you see that? Do you want to share a life with that kind of a person? Aren't you afraid?"

"Why should it surprise you that you are violent? Do you think that you are better than people who aren't violent? Are you above being violent?"

"I hate my violence!"

"You also love it."

"I don't want to love it."

"Then don't love anything. Don't love me. Don't love the trees. Just hate yourself, and they have won."

Max takes out the gun from the dresser drawer. "Here, shoot yourself. Kill yourself. Let them live so you can maintain your 'goodness'. Go to your Heaven that you have to die first to get into. Walt Disney will bless you."

"Don't make fun of me."

"If you say you are the guilty party, then you are an idiot, and I will make fun of your stupidity."

"Don't call me stupid!"

Max takes a chair that's next to the night table and throws it against the wall.

"Then don't BE STUPID!"

"Don't call me stupid!"

She throws the night table at Max. Max grabs her by the shoulders and throws her on the bed. He starts out the door.

"Max! Don't go anywhere!"

Max turns around and looks at her. Her face is soft. He goes to her, and they make love in the mess they have made.

But the issue remained knotted and destructive. They had their passion, but the passion's energy was drained by doubt, by confusion. The 'project' dominated their lives. Chrystal's face was tense.

"You want me to get this over with. I feel you are pushing me to do it. Maybe I don't have the right. Just because I want to, maybe even need to, doesn't erase my being a part of what happened. I could have prevented it. I could have gotten out of there."

"Do you really feel you are responsible, or are you saying that because you can't stand being helpless? You would rather be guilty than helpless. When that bastard held you, you were helpless. Admit that he had you. Now you can have him."

"Yes, he had me, but I let him have me. I didn't take care of myself."

"Why the hell should you have to take care of yourself? Do you want to go around looking over your shoulder, wondering if someone will rape you? Is that a life? If you don't want to, that's OK; but if you think you don't have the right to, if you think you have some moral obligation to this scum, that's something else. Are the victims always wrong? Must a generation of victims excuse Nazis because they didn't dream that the bastards would want to annihilate them, because they didn't just leave everything they owned and escape with their lives, leave their homes and their valuables, just protect themselves, take care of themselves. Are victims, even in some small way, responsible for their being murdered?"

"Is that what this is all about, Max? Your anger about the Holocaust?"

"I want to make life dangerous for murderers and rapists. I'm not a fiery angel standing guard at the gates of Eden, but I am a simple guy wanting to protect someone I love. To me *you* are Eden. This bastard wanted to break back into Eden. In his stupid sick mind, he thought you and every other woman he had violated was his ticket back to innocence. I didn't violate anyone. I have no apology to make. I have my issues with evil, and maybe I can be as evil as the next guy, but when someone needs a victim to satisfy some sick need, they will make a horrible mistake to choose me or mine. I would have killed the bastard long ago, but this may not be what you need, my love, to shoot some meaningless pervert. This is your call. I only want you to be free to do what is right for you."

"I believe you, my darling, and I'm thankful to you. I don't know. I just don't know."

"The question is not if you are violent. The question is, do you have the *right* to be violent? Even the Judeo-Christian God slaughtered populations. Violence is a part of what we are."

"Christ gave us another option. Just leave the syndrome of violence. Let us be led by trees and simple lilies. The option will take us into a future. Violence will bear violence."

"Love bears violence too, maybe even more violence. Look what happened to Christ. Look what happened to every apostle of love. I used to live in Little Italy, and in Little Italy nobody stole anything, either because they had self-respect, or because they were afraid they might get their thumbs cut off. For the would-be victim, it's all the same. It's not *why* he or she gets home safe. It's *that* he or she gets home safe. I'll be as happy as anybody when we don't need to live out our violence, but I refuse to play like it's not part of us, and maybe a positive part of us. If you don't have the need to do this, I respect that. If you do have the need to do it, I respect that too."

"Max, I'm afraid of my violence, you enjoy yours."

"I am who I am, Chrystal. Maybe there are many people in us. Maybe we have lived many lives, and these lives are still alive in us. It is wrong to deny them. The killer in you has been awakened. You can choose the killer's solution or reject it, but denying the killer will only make you sick. My tender, loving killer, I love you and everyone you are."

CHAPTER 6

Max got a call from a Mr. Robins on his answering machine. It seems that Mr Robins was starting a Summer Opera Company and wanted Max to be a part of it. He remembered the Traviata at the Providence Town Playhouse. Would Max be interested? Well, do Hasidic bears put on tefillin in the woods? They meet for an Italian lunch across from Lincoln Center, and the wine was right. The operas would be 'Tosca', 'Carmen', and they would open with 'La Traviata'. The season would be called 'Three Dangerous Dames'. Max was to direct 'Tosca' and, of course, 'La Traviata', which would open the summer festival. Mr. Robins was interested in the 'dark' Violetta, Chrystal somebody. He couldn't remember her last name, but he had the program at home. He wanted to know if Max agreed, and if he knew how to locate her. Max said he would look into it. The dinner conversation that night between Max and Chrystal was interesting.

First they opened the champagne. Then they had roast duck from the Chinese restaurant across the street. There was one problem. Chrystal was happy for Max, but she didn't want to sing.

"Max, you know I can't sing Traviata or anything else. Every time I open my mouth to sing, I get sick at my stomach. I'm happy that I can love you. I'm content with that. Let's not go for more right now."

"We have time. The season starts in July. We have about eight months. I'll tell Mr. Robins that I haven't found out where you are yet. We'll hold the decision open. If you feel it's not right, then don't do it."

"It's a big chance for you. You don't need my problems."

"I need a great Violetta, and that's what you are, but I also need for you to be happy and hungry and full of champagne. Beviam!"

Chrystal moved out of her Village apartment and moved in with Max. They had something that both very much wanted, a home, a home together. The apartment took on that mixture of a woman's home, with pictures hanging on the walls and a man's home, with things out of place, unless one understood some masculine inner logic, that is, Max's inner logic. A comfortable tension developed, which allowed for mutual respect and mutual space. The 'project' went on the back burner but remained at some subconscious level, a part of the fundamental structure of their relationship.

Christmas festivities rolled over New York, dominating every New Yorker's mind if they liked it or not. Yule Time is a jolly time, but it also can be a painful time in New York. The issues of family and the issues of pure and simple financial condition are thrown into everyone's face. Merchants proclaim that love is a purchasable commodity and outdo their last year's efforts to make their point, while, in the same season, a worldwide collective effort is made to acknowledge human sanctity. Even wars manage a breather for a few days. The original Yule homage to Nature's magic and unbounded splendor is alive in the total trust which shines from children's faces, and, as so often happens in this struggling world, it is the child who restores the order adults seem intent on disturbing. The ancient Yule Gods passed the chalice to the simple child. It is with child trust in each other that Max and Chrystal celebrate Christmas, and thus did they ride the camel through the eye of the Yule Time needle.

And so the old year poured into the new. Not everyone had the luck of love to ease them into winter's January. Chrystal and Max had a neighbor. He fancied himself a writer, not so much because he wrote, but because he drank and raised hell in the middle of the night. Great writers were supposed to do that in order to free the genius in their subconscious. Max and Chrystal's bedroom was separated from the genius's cauldron of drunken inspiration by a thin wall. Max pounded on the wall at three in the morning, trying to let the writer know that he was disturbing their sleep. This only brought about more noise. At one point Max called the police, who came and knocked on the door with a billy club, informing the writer that he was disturbing the peace and must keep it down. This worked for a little while but made the tension between the neighbors even worse. Max and the would-be Hemingway found themselves in the elevator one afternoon. A few words were exchanged and the writer punched Max in the nose. The writer was well over six feet tall and was both muscular and fat. Max didn't really have a fair chance in a fair fight. When the elevator reached their floor, they went their separate ways, one smiling and feeling smug and the other feeling a little sick and furious. When Chrystal came home from work that evening, she, of course, noticed Max's swollen face and was frightened. Max tried to console her.

"He's just a drunken asshole, not important enough to get upset about."

Chrystal's darkness moved into her face.

"I know all about drunken assholes."

"He's made his point. Maybe he'll cool down."

"I don't want to live in fear and anger. We've called the police. Do you want to bring charges against him?"

"There were no witnesses, just the two of us in the elevator. He would just claim self-defense."

"Right, a fucking giant defending himself against a guy your size. Max, he better leave us alone. I don't know what we can do, but I do know that he doesn't know what he is getting into with us. I hope this problem disappears."

"I'll talk to the landlord, let him know what's going on. Maybe that will shut him up. Are you hungry? Forget this asshole. You want to go to the Chinese tonight?"

"I'm not hungry."

Max and Chrystal stayed home that night. They were quiet. Around midnight they went to bed and didn't make love. In her sleep, Chrystal found herself in the Alaskan forest. The snow-covered trees extended onto the white sky, laying on top of it. The forest was above the clouds, and she was above the forest, her face burned by a white sun.

She began to spin and fell into a blue-green pool of warm water. She sank deeper and deeper and came to rest in a yellow valley covered with soft green earth. She stood up. Her naked body was draped in emerald velvet, a priestess, holding a silver chalice filled with dark blood. She raised the chalice above her head and poured the blood onto the soft earth, returning the blood to its rightful home. A drum began to sound from some distant drummer who lived in the earth's underworld. She was awakened by Max, who was beating against the bedroom wall.

"Shut the fuck up!"

The writer was roaring drunk and screaming his usual nocturnal ritual.

"Max, what's the matter?"

"The son of a bitch is at it again. Goddamned son of a bitch!"

Max got out of bed and put on his blue jeans. He went to the closet and got a lead pipe, which was there from his construction days. He went to the writer's door and pounded on it with the pipe. The drunken writer opened the door and Max hit him in the face with the pipe. The writer covered his face and Max hit him on his legs and kneecaps. The writer fell, and Max dropped the pipe and began to hit the writer with his fists. The writer pushed Max away and grabbed the pipe from the floor. He managed to stand up. He held the pipe over his head and yelled,

"I'M GOING TO KILL YOU, YOU SON OF A BITCH!"

Suddenly the writer stopped. Chrystal, dressed in her nightgown, was standing in front of him, holding the silver weapon in both hands, arms outstretched. The weapon was pointing at the writer's face, but it was her eyes that stopped him, not the weapon. Her eyes were ice cold with just a touch of joy. She only needed a small move from him, a small reason to blow his horrible face away. She seemed almost to ask him to give her a reason to pull the trigger. The writer was terrified, afraid to breathe, so that she might misinterpret his movement. Max slowly stood up. He watched the frozen writer and his Chrystal. He asked softly, "Do you want to kill him?"

The writer mumbled, "Please."

Chrystal began to breathe slowly. "Put the pipe down."

Her voice was out of place in this violence. It was a young woman's voice, gentle, like a priestess instructing a novice. The writer slowly laid the pipe on the floor. Chrystal slowly lowered the weapon. Max spoke.

"I could use a beer. It's four in the morning and I could use a beer. Why don't we go to our place and have a beer."

Chrystal agreed.

"Great idea. What's your name?"

"Patrick."

Max picked up the pipe, like someone cleaning up after a job.

"You want a beer, Patrick?"

"Great, that's a great idea."

They all went into Max and Chrystal's apartment. Patrick began to relax.

"You guys are some neighbors."

They drank until around eight. Then Patrick left, and Max and Chrystal crawled into bed. There was no more trouble from Patrick. On the contrary, they all became good neighbors. Before Max and Chrystal fell asleep, Max mumbled,

"Darling, you saved my butt tonight."

"That's because I love you."

Max suddenly sat up. He got out of bed and took the weapon out of the night drawer.

"Chrystal, there're no bullets in the gun."

"I don't need bullets. Good night, darling."

"Good night."

A letter came in the mail. It had no return address, but it did have a postmark, Sweetwater, Alabama. Inside was a newspaper article. 'A man was found shot dead in a subway in Chicago. The killing was reported as drug-related. The man was identified as a Mr. Roger Jones.' With the newspaper article was a piece of writing paper, on which 'GOOD WORK' was typed. That was it. Max and Chrystal were stunned. Obviously this guy had had enemies. In all honesty, both Max and Chrystal were relieved, but somewhere inside, they were disappointed. Chrystal felt that her choice had been taken away. This guy had become her spiritual property. She wanted to feel as if she had power over his life. He was around until she shot him. Then, and only then, was he gone. For her, he was still alive in some unfinished space in her mind. Her right hand kept pulling an imaginary trigger. She felt cheated by fate, and at the same time, she felt freed from the constant feeling of a weight hanging over her head. She could go about her life, freed from the 'project'. Or could she? The decision to take dominion over her life's choices gave her a sense of power. It was as if she had created a world, and then on the seventh day, the day of rest forced itself on the goddess. She was thrown out of the celestial heights and regained her helpless identity, a mere human. Max also felt cheated, but the central issue for him was Chrystal. She had fought to overcome being a victim, and she was winning. She was coming into a power, beautiful to behold. He admired her natural strength, her confidence. It was not the killer in her that wanted to be free. It was the goddess. She had a goddess in her, but gods and goddesses often confuse themselves with the infinite energy which sustains them. They are the result of their strength but not the cause of their strength. If they begin to doubt their magic, they can fall into the darkness that was part of Chrystal's character, the constant rising toward the sun and then falling away from it. The sea in which Chrystal swam was an accepting sea. It sustained her in both good and bad weather, but coming to this knowledge can be an entire life's work.

Winter was ebbing away. Spring moved closer. The time was coming around for decisions to be made about 'La Traviata'. Chrystal had made no mention of her intentions since the first discussion several months ago. Max had been in contact with Mr. Robins to discuss the summer festival but avoided any casting discussions. Max broached the subject to Chrystal.

  "It's time, the walrus said."
  "To speak of Traviata?"
  "Right."
He was used to her reading his mind.

"I thought I might give it a try. I called up Doris and set up a coaching with her. I wanted to wait to see how it goes, before I talked about it with you, have something definite to talk about, before I start getting everybody's hopes up. I haven't been on the stage for almost two years, and Traviata isn't exactly 'Melancholy Baby', but it's not the voice I'm worried about. I'm not sure I won't fall apart in the middle of the show. I don't have my stage legs. I'm not used to being so vulnerable. It's one thing to be vulnerable with a weapon in your hand, and it's another to be out there naked, nothing to fall back on if something goes wrong. What if I lose it, Max? I can't stand being helpless. I'm not sure I want to take the risk, not for me and also not for you. This is important for you, Max. They'll say we live together, so I got the role, but I can't sing it. You know this business. They'll come after you as much as they'll come after me. I don't know if I can cope with this whole thing. Why put myself through this hell? We have a lot. Why push it?"

"Work with Doris. Then we'll talk. Is that OK? See how you feel after you sing a little. If you like the idea, good, if not, also good. How's Chinese tonight?"

"What's with you and Chinese?"

"It's like making love with you. I get hungry an hour later."

"You got the chopsticks, " she said as she moved toward the bedroom.

Chrystal sang like a flying bird. At the beginning it was a little stiff, but when she warmed up, it was the singing of someone who had missed singing.

Muscle memory is a kind of a miracle. The singer takes a deep breath and leaps into sound-space. Hunger for that sensation of vibrations buzzing through her body, strong emotions rising up in her breast, being lost in the pain and pleasure of Violetta's tragic drama drove Chrystal back into a world she had been torn out of. This role was hers. Singing was hers. Her life was hers. When the coaching was over, Chrystal went into the hall of the apartment building. She pushed the button for the elevator. Her knees buckled and she wept. As she was on her knees, the elevator opened and an elderly woman stepped out.

"Did you lose something?" she asked in a kind voice.

Chrystal looked up, her eyes shining.

"No, I found something."

She walked the ten blocks home. It was as if she had just finished a performance at the Met. She would sing the Traviata. She and Max would work together, and they would continue the journey they had started what seemed like a hundred years ago. She stopped in a wine store and bought a bottle of champagne. She continued walking up the street. Suddenly she felt as if someone were watching her. She stopped and slowly turned around. The sidewalk was filled with people. No one seemed to be paying any special attention to her. She continued on up Broadway.

Chrystal entered her building. She looked down the street before she unlocked the entrance door. It was a reflex look. Everyone who enters a building in New York throws a glance behind himself before he unlocks the entrance door. Is someone standing too close? Does someone else also want to enter with you? Normal questions, nothing to feel funny about. Tonight will be a really special celebration. Chrystal looked at her watch. Max will be home in about two hours. Tonight will be a steak night. Steak, champagne, wine, the works. There are two beautiful steaks in the freezer. Chrystal is singing softly to herself, something she hasn't done in a long time. The telephone rings. Chrystal is startled. She grabs the phone. "Hello?" No one answers. "Hello? Hello, is someone there?" No answer. Then 'click'.

Chrystal goes back to getting dinner ready. Salad, a good fresh salad. She looks through the refrigerator. She takes out some tomatoes and onions. The phone rings again. Chrystal grabs the phone. "Hello! Hello? Who did you want to speak to?... Hello. Cut the crap!"

She slams the phone down. She goes over to her record collection and puts on 'La Traviata'. The orchestra music fills the apartment, and memories come pouring back, memories of her tour through Canada and Alaska. She hadn't played the 'La Traviata' record for over two years. Visions of snow-covered plains passed before her eyes, memories of being cold while riding in the bus. Sometimes it took a while to warm the bus up. Memories of missing Max, a person she really barely knew in those days. They had worked together, slept together and talked long distance together, but compared to now, they were just good friends in those days. Compared to now, they really didn't know each other. The music brought back the Native American reservation performance. She had promised to bring Max some moose meat. She would surprise him with moose meat. You could get it in New York. You could get anything in New York. The music brought back Chicago. The telephone rang.

"God damnit! Who is it?!" Again, no answer. "Answer me, you son of a bitch!" Chrystal began to panic. She was frightened. Someone was stalking her, wanting to hurt her. The phone rang again. Chrystal went to the closet where Max kept the lead pipe. She took it out and began smashing the telephone. "You son of a bitch! You Goddamned son of a bitch!"

She was crying hysterically when Max came in. She looked up at him.

"I can't do it, Max! I can't do it!"

Chrystal told Max about the coaching, about how wonderful it was to sing again. She told him about what a joy it would be to be working again, to be working together. Then, this telephone thing.

Max tried to calm her.

"Chrystal, it's just some nut. He saw your reaction. That's just what they like, these nuts."

"That's the point, Max. My reaction. I flipped out. I can't deal with threats, real or imaginary. I thought after the coaching I was all right. If I did something like that in a rehearsal or, God forbid, in a performance, I mean, I just don't trust myself."

"Chrystal, you are a passionate woman, so you got mad, so you break a few phones, so what? Before I met you, my life was nothing but chaos. That has a good side. A little chaos doesn't bother me. Life isn't always so simple. At some point we have to throw away our Little Orphan Annie badges.   Life is not some Hollywood movie. Actually you did us a favor. We definitely won't be disturbed by any phone calls tonight. Now, I'm hungry and I'm thirsty and I love you, and I'm not sure in which order."

"You're not sure in which order?"

"I think I'll have the champagne first."

"You'll have the champagne first?"

Chrystal walks to the refrigerator. As she does, she takes her clothes off. She stands naked with the bottle of cold champagne in her hand.

Max changes his order.

"Fuck the champagne."

"Fuck the champagne?"

They have one hell of a dinner.

The next morning Max and Chrystal had a talk.

"Chrystal, I want you to sing the Traviata. Your voice is back, and you seem to really want to do it. I know you are not over the Chicago thing and that you are not secure, but show me an opera singer who is secure. I'm making a purely, well almost purely, professional decision. If you choose not to sing it, I will respect that, and we won't mention it again. I've got to give Robins a cast list. What do you say?"

"You know the risk."

"That's right."

"You're willing to risk it?"

"That's right."

Chrystal went to her dark place in her mind. She took a deep breath.

"OK."

Max kissed Chrystal gently.

"OK. Let's get a new phone. We've got some calls to make."

Chrystal went to work, getting the role in shape. Max met with Robins and informed him that he had found 'the dark Violetta', and they went about casting the rest of the opera. There was also the question of 'Tosca', the other opera Max would direct, but that could wait a little while. They still had a few months, but Robins needed a few things in place so he could put the whole project in motion. It was interesting for Max to hear the word 'project' used in such a positive context.

So life was moving along pretty smoothly. For the first time in Max's life, he had order and chaos in balance. He had gotten into the 'voice-over' business; he had a decent speaking voice, and Chrystal was still doing temp work, so they had money. Max was home studying a script for a voice-over assignment, and Chrystal was at work. The phone rang. Max answered in his voice-over voice.

"Hello."

The voice on the other end was raspy.

"What happened to your phone?"

Max's voice quickly became normal.

"Hello. Who's this?"

"Hello, Max. How you doin'?"

"Fine. Who's this?"

"Don't worry who this is. A mutual acquaintance ran into some bad luck. It seems he had some dealings with your girlfriend, and some questions were asked, so I put two and two together, so that's why I'm calling. This unfortunate owed me some money, and it looks like you and your girlfriend inherited the debt."

"This is all very fascinating, but I'm busy, so fuck off."

"Max, don't say 'fuck off'. I understand your bein' pissed off at this guy, but business is business. You owe me thirty thousand bucks. Max, think about it. Don't make me go into detail."

"Look, if this a joke, you're good, whoever you are. But if this is some kind of threat, you can shove it up your ass. I don't know what the hell you're talking about, and I'm busy."

"Chrystal isn't busy, Max. I could have discussed the situation with her, but I thought it would be the proper thing to wait and discuss it with you. But if you give me bullshit, I'll discuss it with her. That would be unpleasant. You see, Max, I'm not without some sensitivities. You got lucky with this bum, but don't push it. Thirty thousand, and the whole thing is over."

"Look, number one, I didn't have anything to do with the bum you're talking about. If he got into some trouble, then that's his problem. I hope he fries in hell, but I didn't have anything to do with him."

"So why you asking questions about him? I want my money, Max."

"I don't have thirty thousand dollars."

"You're a Jew. You'll get the money."

"Look pal, you're barking up the wrong tree. I asked questions, because I wanted to blow the bastard's brains out, but somebody beat me to it.

Now that's the story, so look somewhere else for your fucking money."

"Don't push your luck, Max. I know where I got to look for my money. I'll call you in a few days. I'm patient, Max, until I'm not patient. Calm down and get the money. We'll talk."
Click.
Max had to think. Number one, he couldn't tell Chrystal about this, not now, maybe later but not now. Number two, this guy wasn't interested in if Max did the shooting or not. He was interested in the angle, that's all. When questions had been asked, Chrystal's name became known. This guy figured whoever shot this bastard might have done it as a revenge. The little lady herself might have done it, so maybe find the lady, maybe find the shooter. Harry didn't know that the bastard had big gambling debts, didn't figure on this possibility. But this latest scumbag wasn't interested in getting even, so it didn't matter if he was right or wrong about Max. It was a simple case of extortion. He could scare Max into giving him some money. Max was a Jew and supposed to have money. That was what it was all about. Number three, Max couldn't give him the money even if he had it, because the price would just keep going up until Max was bled dry. This was theoretical anyway, because Max and Chrystal had no money, period. Now there was number four, this guy couldn't go back to Chicago without the money. People there were waiting on a cut. Maybe go to the police, report an attempted case of extortion, a threat to Chrystal's and his lives. Till now no threat had been made. The whole thing might bring Chrystal into danger, either from

these gangsters or from the law. He and Chrystal had made some illegal inquiries through Harry. So the whole thing just didn't look good.

Chrystal came home feeling great. She had had a coaching after work, and that always gave her an extra burst of energy, as if she needed it. "Max, I got a surprise for you. Remember the performance we did at a Native American reservation? Remember I said I would bring you some moose meat? Voilà!"

She pulled out a plastic bag which contained moose meat. "I went to Citarella's on Seventy-Fourth, and they had it."

She had expected him to leap around like an Indian brave, do a war dance and drag her off to his tepee. Instead he said 'great' or 'wow' or something. Maybe he was tired. People get tired, but Max was not people.

"What's up, sweetheart?"

"Nothing, darling. I'm just a little preoccupied. Geniuses are like that, you know. Can one become a knight if you live in America? Do you want to become a knightess?"

"I think it is a dame."

"Darling, you are a dame. Is moose meat kosher?"

"Sure. You just have to circumcise the moose."

"Actually that's what's preoccupying me. There's this moose I want to circumcise."

"Why do I feel like you're not joking?"

"I'm joking, darling. Just take a good look at a moose, and you'll see I'm joking."

"So who's the guy you want to circumcise?"

"It's nothing, just the set designer. He wants some cold abstract kind of set. How was the coaching?"

"Good, Max, real good."

"How 'bout a shot of the Jack?"

Max pours himself a stiff Jack Daniel's. He gets a glass for Chrystal.

"You want a drink?"

"Just a light one. What kind of set does he want?"

"German Expressionist set. Cold."

"Max, did you get any phone calls today? That nut call again?"

"No nut calls. That guy's moved on to some other number. He had his fun with us. He's moved on."

"I'll get the moose started. If he, or anybody else calls, you tell him we got moose, and you don't mess with the moose."

Max looks at his glass of Jack Daniel's.

"That's right, you don't mess with the moose."

A few days went by before Max got another phone call.

"Hello, Max. How ya doin'?"

"You got a name?"

"Chicago. Call me Chicago. Your girl there?"

"She's at work."

"Good. We can talk. Boy, this city sucks. I'm getting homesick, thinking about getting back.

We got to wind up our business, Max. I got to get back."

"Look, I don't have that kind of money. There's no way I can get a hold of thirty thousand dollars."

"I don't need to hear this bullshit. Today's Tuesday. I'm comin' over there Friday. Three o'clock. See ya Friday, Max." Click.

Max's mind was going over every possibility. He couldn't borrow the money from the bank. He had absolutely no collateral. Maybe Jose could help him. He could get it from the street, but the interest would be exorbitant, and he would really be in the devil's clutches. Jose would want to 'lay the guy flat'. He was being sucked into a chaos that had no end. Even if he got the money, it was just the beginning. This shit would go on forever, and Chrystal would get caught up in the mess. She already was. He needed a drink. By the time Chrystal came home, he had had several.

Bourbon can be like a thermometer. One drink can mean that things are good, and you are about to have dinner. Two can mean the same thing. Three, or let's say four, can indicate temperature. Chrystal didn't ask too much because Max didn't volunteer too much. She trusted Max, so she figured he had his reasons, and it wasn't a set design. Max was not talking because he wanted to protect her. Against what? Was someone against her singing Traviata? Did someone want another Violetta? Max had cooked a simple pasta for dinner, garlic and pepperoncini briefly fried in olive oil, green salad, red wine. Chrystal quietly got to the point.

"Max, has anyone made an objection to my singing Violetta? Anyone against the idea?"

"What? Chrystal, are you nuts? I'm sorry, darling. I've had a few, but that's really coming from left field. What in God's name makes you ask a question like that?"

Chrystal immediately saw she was thinking in the wrong direction.

"I'm sorry, Max. Really. You've got a lot on your mind, and I'm bothering you with some stupid singer insecurity bullshit. This set designer. Is he really bugging you?"

Max poured them both some wine.

"Yes. We're going to get together Friday afternoon. He's coming over around three. You're working Friday, right?"

"I'll get home around six, six-thirty. Will he stay for dinner?"

"No. No, he won't stay for dinner. Darling, I got to zip uptown tonight for a while. You remember Marco? He knows some singer Robins wants in the festival. I want to have a talk with Marco, see what he thinks."

Max abruptly got up from the table, grabbed his coat.

"See you later."

He went out the door. When the door closed, Chrystal was still sitting at the table. She mumbled, "See you later."

She stared at Max's empty plate and empty glass of wine. When she heard the door close, the whole thing became clear to her. There was a major threat going on, a threat to both of them, a life threat.

Friday, Max had a meeting. Friday the thing would be resolved.

Max walked out into the night. He had no intention of going to Marco's. He thought he might try to look up Jose, but that idea was quickly dropped. He just needed to be alone, to walk around, try to think. He went down by the Hudson. People were walking their dogs. They all seemed so peaceful, so safe. He fantasized having a husky dog, a savage son of a bitch that would tear this Chicago bastard to spreads on command. Maybe he could reason with him. He had to protect Chrystal. He could only wait and see what happens, see this guy face to face and just see what happens.

Friday morning, Chrystal got up to go to work. Max was still sleeping. He had had a sleepless night.
Chrystal spoke softly. "Good morning, my love. Sleep, sleep. I don't know what's wrong, but I do know one thing, you're not alone. Whatever it is, we'll get through it together. As long as I'm alive, you're not alone. We will do what we have to do. We'll do it together."
She got dressed. She went to the night table and quietly took the weapon from the drawer. She loaded the weapon and put it in her handbag. She looked at Max's sleeping body. "I'll see you later."
She turned and went to work.

Max woke up around twelve. He made coffee and waited. At three o'clock there was a knock at the door. Max went to the door and opened it. There stood a huge man with a grey face.

"Hello, Max."

"Come in."

The man came in. The two of them stood in the middle of the living room. The man's eyes were darting around the room.

"You alone?"

"Yes, Chrystal is at work."

"That's smart. You got my money?"

"We can talk about this."

The man hit Max in the face with the back of his hand. Max fell backwards. The man took a pistol from his coat pocket. He put it in Max's face. "Look, you fucking Jew. I want my money. What you got here?"

He walked through the apartment looking for valuables. He looked in the kitchen, throwing plates from the cabinet, spilling sugar on the floor. Max felt helpless. The man went into the bedroom and started throwing Chrystal's underwear out of the drawers. He was looking for jewels, anything. Max went to the closet and got the lead pipe. He was afraid the man would find the weapon in the night drawer. The man was ignoring Max, all the time throwing things around the room and cursing. "Where the fuck is some cash! Where do you hide the fucking cash?!"

Max came up behind the man and swung the pipe as hard as he could against his back. Max couldn't reach his head. It was like hitting a sack of flour. The man spun around. He was furious. He grabbed Max by the throat and put the gun in his face. "You goddamned fucking Jew!"

Max hit the man in the face with the pipe. The man was stunned. He stepped back. With his free hand he felt the side of his face, where the pipe had opened his skin. His hand was bloody. "You goddamned son of a bitch!"

Chrystal stood in the open doorway. She held the weapon with both hands, arms outstretched, pointing the weapon at the man. The man lunged at her. Her first bullet entered the man's stomach, the second entered his chest, the third his face. Chrystal and Max stood staring at the dead man lying on the floor in front of them, the man who had said his name was Chicago.

OPERA SINGER KILLS INTRUDER. SAVES LOVER!

The Free Press ran a story, also The Times. It was on the Evening News. Chrystal and Max had become famous. An investigation was launched, and questions were asked. Had either Max or Chrystal known the intruder? Were either of them ever in Chicago? Max said he had never been to Chicago. Chrystal had been there briefly after touring with the Canadian Opera. Did she know anybody in Chicago? Only a few people connected with the opera company. Max said that he thought it was a case of mistaken identity. He told the police what occurred.

"He kept shouting, 'Where's the money, you fucking Jew!' Somehow, he thought I was rich. I'm Jewish, but I'm not rich. I wish it were that simple. If Chrystal hadn't come home just at that moment, if she hadn't done what she did, I would be a dead Jew. I think he thought I was someone else."

The investigator asked quietly,

"There is the question of the handgun used by Miss Bergmann. Where did she obtain a handgun? Does she have a license?"

Max explained.

"I'm a director. I will direct a production of 'La Traviata' this summer with the Summer Opera Company. Part of my concept is that Violetta, the role that Chrystal will sing, always carries a handgun with her for protection. She plays a courtesan whose life is always in danger in spite of the luxury she is surrounded by. The gun makes her feel safe. Unfortunately, it does not protect her from tuberculosis. I wanted Chrystal to get used to having a handgun; it's part of my Stanislavski training, so I obtained one from a guy in Harlem. I used to live in Harlem, and I knew this guy from the street who could get me one. I never knew his name. I just knew he could get me one. It was just a cheap gun. It cost about fifty dollars, really just a prop. We kept it in a drawer. I never dreamed we would need it."

The investigator addressed Chrystal.

"There is something else. Records show that you were hospitalized in Chicago as a result of a burglary attack."

"Yes, I was attacked as I was entering my hotel room. A Caucasian man. He beat my face and I passed out. He was never arrested."

"Do you see a connection between that incident and the recent incident?"

Chrystal thought a moment.

"It never occurred to me. No, I can't see any connection. This man I shot was nothing like the one who attacked me in Chicago. I had never seen the man I shot, never in my life. I regret the taking of a human life, but to be honest, I had no choice. In fact, in view of these attacks, I would like to apply for a license to legally own a handgun."

The inspector coolly watched Chrystal as she made her statements. After a few minutes he spoke.

"I think we can help you out with that."

Max and Chrystal were shown some mug shots. Among the shots was a photo of one Roger Jones. Chrystal said that he looked familiar, but she couldn't be absolutely sure. As they left, Max turned and said,

"You guys are invited to the performance this summer."

He was told that they didn't like opera.

The police did expedite the handgun license for Chrystal. They did it for two reasons. One, the man she shot turned out to be a wanted criminal, a certain Paul Harrison, wanted for first degree murder, extortion, drug-dealing and a few other illegal activities, so she had, in fact, done the state some service. Two, because of the deceased's connection with the criminal elements, it was not inconceivable that she might just need a handgun in the future. It was also for this reason that a little slack was allowed regarding the obtainment of the weapon used in the shooting. The police were not overjoyed with Max's business practices, and they had no idea whatsoever who 'Stanislavski,' or whoever was, but his story sounded believable; theatre types were known for being unconventional, and the obtainment of the weapon had most certainly saved his and Chrystal's lives. Max had no record and seemed to be in no way connected with criminal activities. Also it was not as if the NYPD had nothing else to do but go around wrapping up inconsequential loose ends. For the time being, the police were content to accept Max's and Chrystal's statements at face value. All the information regarding the case was duly recorded, and the ongoing fight against crime went its merry way.

Max and Chrystal, on the other hand, found themselves in a Shakespearian dilemma. They had taken a human life, and they had lied to the police. Certainly, they had saved their own lives by shooting this Mr. Harrison; the legal question of who had actually pulled the trigger was a mute question, and certainly they had avoided prosecution by withholding and falsifying evidence regarding events occurring during and prior to the shooting. But all that was a technicality. The real issue was, could Max and Chrystal live with the choices they had made.

"What have I gotten you into, Chrystal? What if I hadn't been in touch with Harry? Just turned the whole thing over to the police and let them handle it?"

"Nothing would have happened, Max. Nothing. Eventually you'd have gotten tired of living with a stone, and I'd be going to a therapist the rest of my life. Maybe eventually, I'd get up the courage to watch an opera on television."

"I've pulled you into my chaos."

"Someone, a person, not a tree, frightened you. I felt that I had to protect you, protect us. I didn't know what to expect that morning when I loaded the gun. I just knew I had to be ready to kill if it was necessary. I didn't decide to shoot the guy that afternoon, I decided that morning when I loaded the gun. The man lunged at me. I saw he was a human being, as stupid and as cruel as he was, he was still a human being, however obsessed by an illusion of omnipotence and however rotten his inner life, the bastard still possessed the human condition; guts and entrails drenched in a raging life force, desperately trying to get from one day to the next. I watched this ill-conceived creature discover its mortality. I saw his suddenly broken face register its own termination. I shot him and died with him. That's how I stayed alive. I died. That's how *we* stayed alive. I don't know if I have the right to take a life. I just know I had to do it."

"When I was a kid in Hebrew school, we used to translate the Torah. There was this phrase, 'Ve'atah timshol. And thou mayest.' When Cain killed Abel, God said to him "Sin croucheth at the door; and unto thee is its desire. 'Ve'atah timshol', and thou mayest rule over it. We have a choice in everything we do."

"But there are the Ten Commandments. Thou shall not kill."

"There are no Ten Commandments. This is a case of a very loose translation of the Torah. There are 'Ten Words'. The Hebrew translates into English 'Decalogue'. If the Bible is meant to be a metaphor for spiritual instruction, it would help if the translation were accurate. I don't think you want me to love my neighbor because I am commanded to. If I love you because I am commanded to, then I'm just obeying orders. That's not my idea of love.

The wisdom of the Torah, as I see it, always allows choice, but we have to have the guts to permit ourselves this choice. By the way, it doesn't say, 'Thou shall not kill.' It says, 'Thou shall not murder.' In the context of the Torah, killing to save an innocent life is accepted."

"Yeah, but the Torah is just a system, Max, a system that is supposed to lead people to a spiritual life, but systems live in the mind, in dialogue and categories. This pure life I'm looking for doesn't think. If I only did things I understood, I wouldn't even be able to take a piss."

"I don't know if we have that option not to think, Chrystal. We're supposed to 'replenish the earth and subdue it', take dominion over matter. We use our brains to do that. Like birds can fly, we can think. If we didn't think, it would be like a bird that never flew, a bird that never was a bird."

"Maybe we have to redefine thinking, because the thinking that's going on these days won't lead to dominion over matter, it will lead to matter's dominion over us."

"Chrystal, you should be a Rabbi."

CHAPTER 7

Max and Chrystal had definitely attained notoriety. Friends called to offer support and to congratulate them for having survived the whole ordeal. Agents were also not oblivious to the potential drawing power the 'dangerous duo' might generate. Patrick, the writer, after judiciously changing the names, had written a short story about a violent night with the 'pipe killers'. So life went on. Max and Chrystal took the whole 'after vibes' period with a grain of salt, but one voice from the past was very welcome indeed. Jose showed up one night. He just popped over to say hello and to show his gratitude for leaving Jose's name out of the story. Max poured Jose and Chrystal a stiff bourbon. He poured one for himself.

"So, how are things uptown?"
Jose enjoyed the Jack.

"Jumpin', man, jumpin'. This new mayor wants to clean up 42nd Street. All the porno action is movin' up town. Chrystal, sweetheart, I never thought you had it in you. That's not a bad thing, it's just that you are as sweet as they come."
Chrystal was modest.

"I'm finding things in me that I never knew were there. I don't really like what I did, but I didn't make this world. He was going to break Max's head. Not while I'm alive. I love my Max. It's just that simple."
Max was proud and gentle.

"I love my Chrystal."

Max did a refill.

"What do you think, Jose? Are we finished with the Chicago crowd?"

Jose wrinkled his streetwise brow.

"There's no money to be made givin' you guys trouble. There's no reason to take the risks. You may not notice, but the cops are keepin' a close eye on the two of you. For the time being you guys are off limits for any moves from Chicago. I think the whole thing will fade away."

Max sipped his bourbon.

"I sure as hell hope so. We want to get on with our lives. We got an opera to put together."

"You better give this fine woman some children, Max. You hear what I'm tellin' you? You got a fine woman. A fine woman."

Chrystal was shy and a little embarrassed. She just smiled.

They got another phone call. It was from the other Violetta, Sandy.

Chrystal answered the phone.

"Hello."

"Hello, Chrystal, it's me, Sandy. You still remember me?"

"Sandy! How the hell are you?"

"I'm doing fine. Still doing a little singing. I got this exercise business. Keeps me pretty busy, but I still keep the voice in shape. Is Max there?"

"Yeah, hang on a minute."

She calls Max to the phone.

"Sandy! Great to her from you. Need a director?"

"Hey, Max. No. That's not why I'm callin'. You remember the fat guy you used to do a little work for, you and the boxer?"

"Sure, Lew. My God, how is Lew these days?"

"He's OK."

"Has he still got that young girlfriend?"

"Lew's got a lot of young girlfriends. But he's got other troubles now. The police have been bustin' his ass. They're trying to connect him to this fat guy, Abe. They're making a tax evasion case against Abe. They've been questioning Lew. They want him to testify that he moved illegal money for Abe. Lew's cool, but Abe is worried. Anyway Abe wants to talk to you, wants you to drop by."

"Sandy, what's this all got to do with you?"

"You remember the guy that financed our opera? He finances a lot of things, including Abe. The Internal Revenue is after them both. My friend is a generous guy, put me in the exercise business, but he can be a mean son of a bitch. Anyway, for all concerned, it would be a good idea if you had a little talk with Abe. It could be very much to your advantage."

"Sandy, I don't want to get mixed up in this. I've been through enough the past few weeks. You probably read about it."

"Max, talk to the guy. Sure I read about it. My heart went out to you guys. I think you're great, both of you. Talk to Abe. Listen to what he has to say. These people can be a great friend and a bad enemy. When you guys gonna join my exercise class? I'll make you a special deal."

"Sandy, I don't want to insult your friend."

"That's right, Max. You don't. I got to run. Love to both of you."

Click. Max put the phone down.

Chrystal saw a familiar look in Max's face.

"What don't you want to get mixed up in?"

"I don't want to get mixed up in anything except you. Some vulgar son of a bitch I used to know wants to meet with me. I'll make it quick."

"We've got to get free from the old chaos. Why can't we just live our lives?"

"I'll make it quick."

Max caught the downtown express. He got out at 42nd and walked to 10th Avenue. It had been a long time since he was in that neighborhood. Things had changed. The new mayor was keeping his promise. All the old porno movie houses were gone. It used to be that you could walk from 42nd and Broadway to 10th Avenue and see just about every form of perversion that exists, drug addicts, every kind of prostitute, the underworld in flagrant glory. As Max walked along his old stamping grounds, all he saw was tourists and things tourists buy. Of course, the present environment, however bland, is preferable to the old days, but Max smiled to himself as he thought, 'I remember it when... .' His appointment with Abe was at six. He was on time. He went up in the elevator just like in the old days. Just like in the old days he knocked at the door. He heard Abe lumbering to the door and heard the old,"Whoth there?"

Abe opened the door, and Max walked into the unforgettable stench of stale sex and perfume. That and, of course, the thick clouds of cigar smoke ended any hope of normal breathing. Nothing had changed in this department. It had been at least seven years since Max had seen Abe, and he didn't look good, not that he ever did.

"Come in, Math. Ith good to thee you. Wanth a thrink?"

"No thanks, Abe. What's on your mind?"

"Thit down, Math. I want to thalk to you. Max, where you throm?"

Max takes a seat and tries not to show the fact that he is on the verge of passing out.

"Where'm I from? From Tennessee. I was born in Chattanooga, Tennessee."

"No kiddin', I didn't know thath. Tennessee? No kiddin'? Thath not what I mean. I mean where are your parenth, your grandparenth from?"

"My grandparents come from Lithuania, from a little village near Vilnius. Why?"

"My grandparenths come from Vilniuth too. We could be family. You could be my nethiew. I could be your uncle. Uncle Abe."

"Could be, Abe. Could be."

"Math, some people may want to asth you thome quethtionth about our bithneth dealingth. Thucking poleeth been getting into my private bithneth. You tell 'em we juth talked about family. You underthand?"

"I understand, Abe. Don't worry."

"Good."

Abe takes an envelope from his pocket and hands it to Max.

"Here'th a little thomthing from Uncle Abe."

110

"No thanks, Abe, it's not necessary."

"Come on. Do me the favor."

"Abe, you make your choices. I make mine. I'm not going to talk to the police, because this cleanup crap is just politics. I got to get to work. Don't worry, Abe. If they ask me questions, I'll think of something. Abe, do you mind if I give you some advice? I mean we're family, right? Do you mind if I give you some advice?"

"What advith?"

"Abe, open a window."

Max left and went back onto the street. The traffic fumes were like pure mountain air. He headed to the subway.

"Hey, Mr. Fagan."

Max turned around. It was the two detectives who had interviewed him and Chrystal a few weeks ago.

"Where you headed, Max? Would you mind coming with us? We would like to ask you a few questions."

They went to the precinct. The two detectives were polite. They offered Max a seat in their office.

"Want some coffee, Max?"

One joked.

"Hey Max, you're not packing a stage prop, are you? How's Miss Bergmann doing?"

"She's doing fine, thanks. We're going into rehearsal in a few weeks, so she's pretty busy."

"Her license will be ready in a few days, but you know you can't use the weapon as a prop in the show."

"I don't think we will use it at all. It will give Chrystal a feeling of security, just to have it around. Thanks for helping with the bureaucratic stuff."

"You mind if we ask you a few questions about your visit this afternoon?"

"Sure. What visit?"

"This afternoon, just before we ran into you. Do you mind if we ask who you were visiting?"

"You mean just before you guys picked me up? Yeah, that was a funny thing. You know, this thing with the shooting, it's made Chrystal and me... not famous, but you know, a little well known. So yesterday a guy calls me, wants to talk about producing an opera. So I go down to meet him. Big fat guy. Weird, anyway, I go talk to him, and it turns out he's the uncle of an old colleague of mine, a woman who sang in the first opera I ever directed. So he wants to finance an opera with her as the leading singer. Well, I had to say no, because the lady can't sing, and that can be very embarrassing for everybody concerned, so I had to say no. Well, he gives me an envelope with ten thousand dollars in it. I had ten thousand dollars in my hands."

Max smiles and takes a dramatic pause. "Ten thousand bucks. It hurt to give it back."

"You ever see this guy before? Ever had any dealings with him? Back when you were doing that opera?"

"I don't remember ever seeing him around. He said he's the girl's uncle. Maybe he was around, but I don't think so. He's fat, really fat and talks funny. If he were around I would remember, but I was pretty busy, you know, directing the opera. He could have been at a rehearsal or something. I don't remember seeing him around."

"He never gave you anything to deliver to anybody, a package or a bag or something?"

"No. You know, when you direct an opera, you don't have time to do errands. It's bad for your image."

"You ever run into a guy named Lewis Brown."

"Lewis Brown? No. Lewis Brown?"

"Right."

"The name's familiar. There used to be this boxer from Connecticut or Maine, somewhere. He was a state champion. I used to box, so I know a few names. You talking about that Lewis Brown?"

"Right."

"I never saw him. It was a little before my time."

"Where did you box, Max?"

"College."

"Where did you go to college, Max?"

"South Carolina. I went to the University of South Carolina. Had ten fights. Won 'em all. I got pretty beat up in the last one, but I won on points. I don't have the right nose for boxing."

One of the detectives looks straight into Max's eyes.

"Max, you know anything about this Lewis Brown or this other guy, the fat one, we would appreciate a call."

"Sure, if I remember anything, I'll call you."

As Max was leaving, the detective with the penetrating eyes calls out,

"Say hello to Miss Bergmann."

"Right, sure thing."

As Max walks out of the precinct, a saying from the Talmud comes into his mind. 'One lie is followed by a thousand lies'. He mumbles, "Boy, ain't that the truth."

"Well, here we are, back in the soup."

With these words, Max walks into their apartment.

"Max, what happened? What did the guy want?"

"What did he want? What did the police want? What about us? What about what WE want? I want a drink."

Max pours himself a few fingers of bourbon.

"You want one?"

"No. What happened?"

"Jose was right. The cops are following us around. I don't mind. It's probably better for us, but why? Is it Chicago, or is it Sandy's nervous sugar daddy? By the way, your license will come through any day. Chaos, chaos. Why always chaos?"

"Jose said that the people in Chicago would leave us alone, and I don't think Sandy's friend would hurt us."

"Tax evasion is serious. I'm sure that's just the beginning. Prostitution for sure. That bunch has a lot to lose."

"Darling, what has all that got to do with you? You weren't involved in any of that mess."

"I have information. I transferred some money illegally. Lew and I would bring little brown bags of non-taxed money to people this Abe guy owed. It had to be non-traceable transactions."

"Is that so serious an offense?"

"No. It's just that I can give evidence that the money was illegally transferred. They can use that to nail this Abe guy and Sandy's friend. Income tax evasion, that's how they got Al Capone."

"So Abe thinks you would give evidence against him?"

"He offered me a bribe, and I didn't take it. That worries him. If I take the money, I'm part of the deal. I'm bought. If I don't, I'm too unpredictable."

"Darling, I'm sorry to bring this up, but Robins called. He didn't know who I was, just thought I was your girlfriend. I didn't say, 'Hello, I'm the dark Violetta. Can I help you?' I said you'd call him when you got in."

"Yeah, we've got to draw up a rehearsal schedule. Chrystal my love, let's forget all about this cops and robbers stuff and go do an opera. It's too late to call him now. I'll call him tomorrow. Boy! What I wouldn't give for a little boredom."

The rehearsals took place in rented rehearsal space at the Ansonia Hotel. The cast and set and lighting designer as well as the producer and the director all met to discuss the basic concept of the opera and the way the director had in mind to present it. Max explained how he would proceed.

"My point of view is that the society in which Violetta lives is a corrupt society. That's why I want to present the opera in our time and in our society. Some of the scenes take place in New York, some on the West Coast, some in Paris, and one in a little mountain town upstate called North Creek. There will be no indication of a specific crime organization like the Mafia or some gangster group. I just want to create an atmosphere which is totally normal and totally evil."

Max then introduced the members of the production team, the conductor and the members of the cast to each other. When he got to Chrystal he smiled

"And this is our Violetta, Chrystal Bergman, who has promised not to shoot anybody."

Chrystal stood up, her face very red. She smiled and, looking at Max, said sweetly,

"I might make an exception."

This whole interchange brought laughter and relief. The 'unmentionable theme' had been mentioned, and the rehearsals could get underway.

The first scene takes place in San Francisco in a very luxurious apartment overlooking the Pacific Ocean. The guests are a mixture of people wanting to get something and people willing to give something for a price, and among the favored forms of barter were women like Violetta, women of great beauty, highly intelligent; women whose sparkling gifts of nature were consumed and thrown away like so many oysters on a half shell. The cast was excited by the approach Max was taking to the opera, and Chrystal was so good that it was scary. The three-week rehearsal period went by like a beautiful dream. Then the whole cast moved to Lake George, New York, where the summer festival was about to begin.

It was a glorious July. The cool sweet air, the mountains, the lake and the music brought out all that is splendid in human beings. Love affairs sprang up like flowers in a children's movie. It was a world so far away from the ugly events of the past few months that Max and Chrystal could completely forget their problems, forget Chicago, forget Abe and Sandy's friend, forget the police. It was in this state of euphoria that Max considered a question that had been turning around in his head. It was their day off. 'Day off' was a euphemistic term for being able to sleep an hour longer. The premiere was a week away and there were a million details to consider, a million minor problems to solve. But nevertheless, Max and Chrystal were having a leisurely ten minutes over a cup of coffee before Max had to go to a production meeting. So, Max being a man of few words, said,

"Chrystal, ah, how do you feel about everything, I mean the way the rehearsals are going?"

"Great, Max."

"I mean, the voice sounds great, I mean, you don't feel tired, do you?

Chrystal tilted her head a little.

"No, Max."

Max fiddled with his coffee cup a little.

"That's great. I've got a production meeting in a few minutes, but I wanted to, well, ask you something. I mean, before I go to the meeting."

Chrystal looked into Max's struggling face. Her eyes filled with warmth.

"What, Max?"

Max looked at her and then at his coffee cup and then back into her face.

"Chrystal, ah, let's get married."

Chrystal took Max's face in her hands.

"Max, yes. Let's get married."

They kissed for hundreds of years, and Max went to the meeting. The meeting lasted for several hours, but Max had no idea of what had transpired at the meeting.

The general rehearsal had gone basically OK. The crew was setting up for the dress rehearsal, the last rehearsal before the opening. The singers were getting into costume and makeup. Max and his assistant were sitting at the director's desk in the middle of the auditorium. The assistant was looking through The New York Times. He was called up to the stage to check a light. Max saw the Times and casually picked it up. He mumbled,

"What's been going on in Sodom and Gomorrah these days?"

The assistant called to him.

"Max, can you take a look at this?"

Max put the paper down and started to go up to the stage. As he laid the paper down, he noticed the name, Lewis Brown, on an inside page.

"Hang on, I'll be right up."

Max looked at the article.

'EX-MIDDLE HEAVYWEIGHT DIES OF HEART ATTACK.'

Max calls up to the assistant.

"Take over. I've got to check something."

Max takes the paper into the lobby of the theatre, where the light is better.

'Ex-boxing champion is found dead in his apartment. Probable cause of death is a heart attack. Mr. Lewis was 58 years old.'

Max mutters, "Heart attack, my ass."

The rehearsal went OK, but Max couldn't concentrate on it. His mind was going a thousand miles an hour. There was no way that Lew could have had a heart attack. He took care of himself. He was always drinking fruit juice, didn't smoke, didn't drink. He watched his weight. No way. He had to keep this to himself for the time being. He had to think. Chrystal was great, a little nervous, but that was normal. The orchestra was a little too loud. He would talk to the conductor. Damn!

The most useless feeling in the world is the feeling a director has the night of a premiere. His work is over. It's done. There's nothing more he can do except suffer and smile encouragingly at all his colleagues. Everybody came on stage just before the first act for the traditional 'it has been great and I love you all' talk. Max left Chrystal alone after a 'break a leg' kiss, so she could concentrate. The issue of Lew's death was forgotten for the time being. Max was wearing a black suit, which only helped him feel even more ridiculous. He wandered around the theatre lobby as the audience gathered. They all seemed friendly enough. How friendly will they be when they realize that what they are watching is not a traditional Traviata? Max has an incredible urge to take an oblivion pill. Eventually the house dims down to half. The house lights slowly dim to darkness, and the conductor makes his entrance. He is warmly greeted with a brief applause and then silence. Max stands at the back of the theatre. Warm, soft, lonely music seeps into the auditorium as if it is a lost wanderer that has stumbled into what it thinks is a shelter. The music suddenly becomes aware that people are staring at it as if it were visible. With a sudden gathering of courage, the music explodes into a wild party, and 'La Traviata' has begun.

The curtain calls were joyous. The cast members each took their bows and were greeted with warm enthusiasm. Chrystal, having the title role, took the last cast bow and modestly conquered the audience. The production staff was warmly greeted, and by the time Max took his bow, he was so high be didn't even hear the applause. There was a party in the foyer, and the summer night washed into morning. The next morning Chrystal and Max woke up lying next to each other. They knew that it was something they would do for the rest of their lives.

The reviews wouldn't be out until the next day. They had the whole day before them. They would do nothing today, absolutely nothing. The next show wasn't until the day after tomorrow. It was that time in the valley of the wave. The waters would gather soon enough, but for now there was peace. Max slowly began to let the reality of the Times article seep into his consciousness. He didn't mention it to Chrystal. Not yet. Let her float. They spent the day walking around the lake and talking about how they wanted to get married. Max offered,

"I guess we go to a marriage bureau. We have to get a license."

"I think we have to take a blood test. You know what I'd like? I'd like Jose to be a witness."

"That's a great idea. When we get back to the City, we'll get everything together."

The reviews came out the following day. They were great. There was a great deal of discussion about the direction, as is the fashion, and for the most part it was very positive. Some of the critics thought it fascinating that Violetta appeared at the beginning of the opera toying with a small revolver, especially since they were very well aware of Chystal's and Max's dramatic life. Some critics found it to be stretching a point that the opera was an indictment against today's social climate. To be honest, Max might never have directed the opera in the way he did, had the whole shooting not occurred. He had told the police that the weapon Chrystal used was obtained to prepare her for this special interpretation. At the time he made that statement, there was no interpretation. Max built the concept around Chrystal's-Violetta's need to have a handgun. The more Max rehearsed the opera, the more he saw that the concept made sense. Everyone agreed that the idea was unique and powerful. The singers were praised, and Chrystal was celebrated. The special dark warmth of her voice combined with her extraordinary stage presence and her vulnerable beauty caused some critics to predict that Chrystal would be the next great Violetta. But for Max and Chrystal, the main thing was that Chrystal was proud of Max, and Max was proud of Chrystal.

Max had a couple weeks off before he would start rehearsals for 'Tosca'. As with 'La Traviata', the preliminary rehearsals would be in New York. When they got back to the City, they went for a marriage license. And, yes, they had to take a blood test. Max looked up Jose, and he was very honored to be a witness.

Max told Chrystal about the Times report, about Lew's 'heart attack' and how he didn't believe the story.

"Max, maybe he had a heart attack. I mean, why in God's name would anyone commit murder just to be on the safe side? Lew wouldn't say anything against this fat bastard. I mean, from what you tell me, Lew was too simple in the head to be dangerous."

"That's the point. Lew didn't have the mental agility to lie. Any good interrogator could have tied him up in knots in two seconds."

"But what has all that to do with us? Do you really think that we're in danger?"

Max was cautious.

"I think it wouldn't hurt to be careful".

A marriage license wasn't the only license Max and Chrystal got. The weapon license was also approved, and they picked them both up on the same day. It made Chrystal feel funny to be finger-printed, photographed and then go get a marriage license. In an operatic way, the whole thing was romantic.

The ceremony was set for 10 o'clock Thursday morning. They were to show up with their witness at City Hall on Wall Street with their license. It was an ungodly hour. The whole thing was ungodly, which is what made it Godly. Anybody who would go through all that bureaucracy must love each other very much. Jose showed up wearing his usual attire plus a tie, which he dug up from somewhere for the occasion. There were several other couples waiting for their turn to be officially bound, and the whole atmosphere was a tender mixture of shy people in a collective privacy.

When it was Max's and Chrystal's turn, the three of them went into a room designated to be the marrying room. An officer of the state spoke to them in somber and sincere tones.

"We are gathered here today to join Max Fagan and Chrystal Bergmann in holy matrimony." He then went on in a matter of fact voice.

"Do you have rings?"
Max answered,

"No, we don't want rings."
They had chosen to forego symbolism. Their statement of love for each other was all they needed. The official was a little surprised. He continued.

"Will the couple then join hands."
Max and Chrystal gave their hands to each other.
The official went on."With the power vested in me, I now pronounce you man and wife. Will the witness please sign here."

He indicated to Jose to sign the marriage document. Jose shyly took a provided pen and signed the document. Max and Chrystal gently kissed each other and then the three of them all put their arms around each other. Then they got the hell out of there.

'Tosca' was Max's next opera. The situation in this opera was not that different from Max's and Chrystal's situation. Two lovers, one a painter, the other a singer, simply wanted to go about their lives loving each other and doing their art. Alas, a villain, a baritone, was intent on destroying the happy couple. In the opera, everybody dies. This detail did not go unnoticed by Max or Chrystal. Of course, what is opera without tragic endings? When the curtain comes down, the singers stand up and take a bow. Opera is not real life. This became Max's concept. Opera would suddenly become real life. The opera would be seen as a rehearsal. The singers would wear normal rehearsal clothes. When they were finished singing, they would break character and stand on the side of the stage and drink coffee and watch the 'rehearsal'. Only the baritone was in 'real life' a psychopath. When the hero, a tenor naturally, was executed, the baritone substitutes real bullets, and the whole cast is horrified to discover that their colleague is really dead. Chrystal's voice was not yet heavy enough to sing the role of Tosca. It a few years it would be. By then, Max would have another idea as to how to stage it. Directors are so creative.

Jose was a welcome guest at the Fagans'. He taught Chrystal how to make soul food. One of Max's favorite dishes was collard greens. He admired Jose's secret recipe.

"I'm from the South, you know. I know all about Southern food, but I never could make it myself."

Jose was proud of his cooking.

"You got to know how to make it to really like it."

"I don't know how to make bourbon, but I sho' like it."

Chrystal was working on the sweet potatoes.

"Jose, what do you know about this Abe guy. Is he a dangerous person?"

"He's nothing. He just works for his boss, runs the houses. They've all moved uptown. Abe's boss is mean. Bad dude. Word is, he's takin' heat. Law's cookin' his ass."

"Max, you told Jose about the bribe?"

"Yeah, the fat guy made an offer. I'm not about to sell 'em out. I just don't want anything to do with them."

Jose agreed.

"You take the money, you implicated."

Max nodded.

"You hear about the boxer? Lewis Brown?"

"Yeah, he was OK, Lew. Used to come up town to that jazz club on 149th. Bring his girlfriends up there."

"You think it was a heart attack?"

"Maybe. Some o' those chicks was pretty young."

"Some o' those chicks could have been working for Abe's boss."

Chrystal puts a plate of spare ribs on the table.

"Max, are spare   ribs kosher?"

"They are when Rabbi Jose makes them."

The rehearsal period for Tosca was over, and the cast moved to Lake George. Max, of course, went with them. Chrystal stayed in New York to keep her hand in the temp business, and she went to Lake George on weekends. Max was busy with the show, but it was really the first time that they were separated since the fateful Canadian Opera tour, and he missed her very much. He was also concerned

125

about her because of the whole Abe business, but they had agreed that they would not let the chaos world intrude on their lives. Chrystal went about her work, kept her voice in shape, and they kept the phone company in business. They didn't make a secret of their marriage, but they also didn't announce it. It was their private thing. That was their style. They were private people. They had their own rules, their own way of doing things. When Chrystal came up the first weekend, Max assembled the cast and introduced her to those who didn't know her from the Traviata. She came to an evening rehearsal. Before the rehearsal began, he said proudly, "Ladies and gentleman, I would like to introduce to you, Mrs. Chrystal Fagan."

There were a few surprised reactions. Several company members knew her, or knew of her, but other than Jose and their parents, no one knew that she and Max had gotten married. They were building their private world, or trying to anyway. Max often thought it must have been wonderful to have lived a few hundred years ago in some Polish village, some little Jewish shtetl, where life was clear and simple when there were no Cossacks around. One could live in a private relationship with Nature or God or whichever Name one wanted to use. This ongoing traffic between one's inner life and the Cosmic Dimensions was protected by traditions and religious laws. Of course one could say it was overly protected, and of course people were people in those days. They gossiped and put their noses into other people's business. Sure, business was business, and there was envy and jealousy and the whole package that makes up human chaos without which, by the way, there would be no opera, no theatre. But among the genuinely learned, there was only one goal, to love and respect the private path between a human being and infinity. It is around this principle that religion was conceived, and when religion is misused, it is this principle which is sullied.

The Tosca premiere was the last premiere of the festival season. The Carmen production had gone well, and Tosca had managed to cause a scandal. For a young director, this was not a disadvantage, but Max was disappointed in the reaction. It had been his intention to tell a story, not to sensationalize the opera. Opera was sensational enough on its own. Mr. Robins was extremely pleased. The festival was a success, and he felt that Max and Chrystal had made large contributions to that success. City Opera had contacted Mr. Robins to make inquiries about taking the Traviata production to New York.

Max had a meeting with the production staff at Lincoln Center where the City Opera made its home. Rehearsals for Traviata would begin in January. Some adjustments had to be made regarding the Traviata set. The City Opera stage was much larger than that at Lake George, and there were a few other pre-production considerations to be discussed, a few items they wanted to clear up before the Christmas season began. Max had a good feeling about the project and about life in general as he walked up the stairs leading from the stage entrance of City Opera to the street. As he was walking away from the theatre, he heard someone call his name. He turned around to see a young man in his twenties smiling and coming toward him.

"Mr. Fagan! You're Mr. Max Fagan, right?"

"Yes?"

"Mr. Fagan, I saw your productions at Lake George this summer, and I really liked them. I'm an actor, I mean, I'm still studying, but I'm thinking about directing. I just wanted to say hello."

"Hey, I'm glad you liked them. Where do you study?"

"American Place Theater. Wynn Handman. You know him?"

"Sure, I know Wynn. I think he's a great teacher."

"I don't want to bother you, just wanted to say hello. Ah, I'm supposed to give you this." He hands Max an envelope.

"What's this?"

"A guy named Abe asked me to give it to you, says it's a Hanukkah present."

"Wait a minute."

Max takes the envelope and looks inside. The envelope contains a thick stack of dollar bills.

"You know this Abe?"

"I run a few errands for him every now and then. Man's got to eat. He asked me to give it to you."

"What's your name? Mind if I ask?"

"Hey, I'm honored. My name's Sammy, Sam Levine. Pleased to meet you."

He puts out his hand. Max takes his hand.

"Sammy, you got time for a cup of coffee?"

"Sure."

They go to a coffee shop on Broadway.

Max and Sammy sit over a cup of coffee and Max tells Sammy a story.

"I used to run a few errands for Abe myself not that long ago. Sammy, Abe is poison. I got myself into a lot of trouble because of this guy. He's mixed up with a dangerous crowd. They'll do you a lot of favors, but one day, and you can count on it, one day they'll present you with the bill. Do yourself a favor and walk away from this shit. Now, I can't take this envelope. I don't have to spell it out for you. You tell Abe you couldn't find me and give him the envelope back. Just tell him you couldn't find me and walk. If I can help you, I will. I'll be working here at the opera. If I can do something, I'll talk to the people here, see what I can do, but Sammy, do yourself a favor, don't get mixed up with these bums."

"What can I say, Mr. Fagan?"

"Call me Max."

"What can I say, Max. I'm grateful. I hear what you're saying. I never saw you. I'll drop the envelope back and say I couldn't find you, and that's it. Max, can I do you a favor? Can I buy you a cup of coffee?"

"It's a deal. Tell me, what did you think about the Tosca?"

They spent an hour or so talking about theatre.

Max came home, wondering what would happen next. The one way they could get at him was Chrystal. With Traviata coming up, she was in no position to be bothered with this chaos. He thought about giving Abe a call, try to reassure him, but one, Abe wouldn't talk on the phone, and two, Abe wasn't the problem. Sandy's friend was the problem. He decided to pay Sandy a visit.

Sandy's studio was on 73rd and Broadway, nice location. He took the elevator up to her exercise club. It was a lavish operation, lots of exercise equipment, lots of mirrors, plush furniture, classy. Sandy was glad to see Max. It had been a long time. She came running over to greet him, the same sunflower blond hair, the same electric blue stretch pants which emphasized her broad beam and the same cobalt blue eyes.

"Maxie, great to see you. You caught me at a good time, not much going on at this hour. In a couple hours, all hell breaks loose here. Come up to the office."

They go up some spiral stairs and into Sandy's office. Again, plush. Red leather furniture, and what every health club needs, a bar.

"Maxie, it's good to see you. Have a seat. How's Chrystal? I'm really happy for her success. I admit I was a little jealous. Hey, that was supposed to be my Traviata. That's life. I'm happy I helped a little. Even helped bring you two guys together."

"I got some news. We're married."

"What! My God! Mazel tov! Married! Congratulations."

"Sandy, we have a problem."

"All married people have a problem."

"No. That's not the problem. The problem is your friend. He's pushing me to take a bribe. To begin with, there's no need. The police have already questioned me, and I told them some cock and bull

130

story, and they believe me. I wouldn't say anything stupid. You know that."

"I know that. He doesn't."

"Can you reason with the guy? He's really getting on my nerves."

"He's not normal these days. The cops are watching everything he does. They questioned me. They're sticking their nose everywhere, looking for anything. They're out to get the guy. He's scared. When he gets scared, he gets mean. I've known him a long time. Normally, he's a pussycat. He set me up here. He'll do anything for a friend."

"Like what he did for Lew?"

"I loved Lew. That broke my heart, and it also scared the shit out of me. I can't talk to him when he's scared. I advise you to take the money. Have a good time and forget it."

"That would make me an accessory to his operations. Sandy, I don't know what to do. I do know one thing. If he harms Chrystal, I'll kill the son of a bitch, whoever he is. I'll kill him."

"I didn't hear that, Max."

"You heard it. Get this guy off my back. Sandy, Chrystal and I have a good life. Things are looking good. Just tell him he's safe with me. There's no need to overreact."

"I'll try, Max. I'll see what I can do."

"You do that, and you got a couple of new clients."

"Give Chrystal my love."

It was a strange Christmas present, a pearl-handled, blue steel handgun. It wasn't as ladylike as they thought it was going to be when they went in to buy it. They had been thinking in terms of something more symbolic than functional, something like a cigarette lighter that could also kill people. But as the moment came closer, the buying moment, the joining of their intention with an action, an action which would have consequence, they thought more seriously. This might turn out to be more than a game or a philosophical statement. The weapon had weight. It had a unique smell. It came with a small holster. The ammunition it required looked serious. One could count on its doing what it was supposed to do. Unless one is a policeman or a hunter, one doesn't go inside a weapon store very often. It is strange to be surrounded by these dramatic, finely tuned objects: handguns, rifles, dormant weapons, not displayed in light, like jewelry or fashion wear but kept in locked glass cases and half shadows. The man who sold the weapon was professional, discreet. Max and Chrystal explained that the purchase was a protective procedure, but no details were volunteered, nor were any required. The salesman seemed to be experienced in his job. As Max and Chrystal left the weapon store down in the stock market district near Wall Street, they felt as if they were emerging from another world. They brought their little package uptown. They put it in the 'gun drawer' and made themselves a stiff drink. Chrystal was full of mixed emotions.

"Do you think we will ever use that thing? It sits there almost like it's a prayer object. We are members of the" (she lowers her voice) "Gun Religion."

Max had had enough Sturm und Drang.

"Let's say it's an expensive paperweight."

Max had told Chrystal about the young man Abe had sent to him, also about Max's visit with Sandy. That's more or less what made them decide to go ahead with the gun purchase. The whole thing was insane. Chaos was having a holiday with them, as if it were an evil spirit which was jealous of the Christmas spirit and wanted a little action for itself also.

CHAPTER 8

Sandy's 'friend' was a slight man. His name was
Sol Deitsch. Short, thin, balding, he looked like a
stick of patient dynamite. Deitsch was born in
Hamburg, Germany. In those early days in
Hamburg, Deitsch had been a somewhat plump
man. He had been in the clothing business,
women's apparel. He had a small, successful
fashion boutique. His wife, Sadie Deitsch, had been
an attractive woman, which was very useful,
because she could model the latest fashion lines.
She helped Deitsch with the store, and in her spare
time she studied music, took singing lessons.

All this came to an end four o'clock one morning in
January, 1938. They were arrested and brought
down to the magistrate, where they were held in
detention for two days in separate cells. On the third
day, they were brought to trial on charges of theft. It
was never made clear to them who exactly had
brought the charges against them, but Deitsch had
his suspicions. A competitive store in the
neighborhood was closely aligned with the
prevailing political trends, and similar inexplicable
events had occurred to business acquaintances of
Deitsch, Jewish business acquaintances. At the trial,
Sadie was put on the stand and was harassed by the
prosecution in an attempt to force her to give false
evidence against Deitsch. The prosecution offered
leniency to Sadie if she cooperated. Deitsch stood
by helplessly as her examination continued. Absurd

charges were leveled against Deitsch, charges including theft and falsification of records. The prosecution threatened Sadie with years of imprisonment unless she 'admitted' her participation in the illegal activities and testified to having witnessed Deitsch's manipulating tax and sales records. Sadie refused to cooperate and was taken from the stand screaming hysterically. When Deitsch took the stand, he remained silent. He didn't utter a sound. His face was frozen. A glare was tattooed into his eyes, a glare which would stay with him for the rest of his life. His examination was an absurd scene. The prosecution began screaming at Deitsch, calling him a Christ murderer, a Jew pig. Nothing could provoke him to speak. Eventually he was escorted from the stand by two policemen and was later taken to a detention center. The center was an improvised affair filled with men, women and children being processed for transportation to various ominous destinations. Chaos and confusion prevailed. The orderly processing of victims of Nazi terror had not yet been perfected. Men were being forced into one line and women and children into another. Some were yelling and crying, others were passive. Policemen and policewomen were trying to retain order, some using force, others trying to persuade the prisoners to remain calm with promises that no harm would come to them. In the confusion, Deitsch calmly walked out a door which led to some stairs leading to the street. He disappeared into the crowded city.

Deitsch walked the streets. He couldn't go to his home even to pick up something, clothes or money or something. He couldn't go to friends. They were surely being watched or being arrested themselves. To survive, he had to start a new way of living, street living. The police had taken his valuables when they arrested him, his watch and cash, even his wedding ring. That fact, the fact that they took his wedding ring had come up in his mind later when he was sitting in his cell. The police told him he would get everything back, but something began to happen to his brain when he remembered about his wedding ring. Sitting there in his cell, his mind felt a needle, and that sharp pain in his mind never left him his entire life. Deitsch stayed away from places that he knew.

He spent the first few days living on a high energy, an energy that blocked fear and hunger and fatigue. The first sign of his physical deterioration was dizziness. He had to sit down. He sat down on the sidewalk. He didn't have his winter coat, only his grey suit and a white shirt. It was cold. He went to the train station to stay warm. When he was normally in a train station, he would stand around without being concerned about where he was standing. He would stand in the middle of the station or maybe look through a magazine at a newsstand, but now people looked at him with a judgmental ugly face when he just stood around. He felt that he was too obvious. Someone might report him to the police. He might be arrested as a vagrant. He mustn't stand out. It could cost him his life. He noticed bums sitting in groups, sitting off to a corner, sitting in small groups. He was getting weak. He had to sit down. He went over and found a place to sit where he could lean his back against a wall. He sat down and fell asleep.

When Deitsch woke up, he was hungry. He could smell wurst cooking. There was a wurst stand nearby with long wursts frying. People would nonchalantly come over and buy a wurst which was placed inside a bun. They would buy a cup of hot coffee or a beer. Deitsch watched the people around the wurst stand as if they were from another planet, a planet he had once lived on, some time in another life. He watched them as if they were a dream he was having. His head was spinning. Suddenly a man noticed that he was late for his train. He left quickly, leaving his wurst half-eaten on the little round table. Deitsch managed to stand up and go to the table. He took the unfinished wurst in his hand. He noticed that the coffee cup the man had been drinking from still had some coffee in it. Deitsch quickly took the cup. It was still a little warm. Deitsch walked back to his place near the wall with his food and slowly ate and drank. Then he fell asleep.

Deitsch woke up. It was about three in the morning. A short square man wearing a black jacket and black pants was standing about six meters from him, talking to some young men. They were just chatting. One of the young men gave the short man some money. He palmed what looked like a 50-Reichsmark note to the man. The short square man gave the young man a small envelope.

Sol thought, 'So that's what drug dealing looks like. Harmless-looking.'

A young girl came over. She chatted with the short square man and handed him money. She casually looked over her shoulder as she gave the man money. She also received a small envelope. The girl looked to be about 14 years old. Sol wondered to himself, 'Where do young people get so much money?' Two bums managed to stand. They went to the dealer. Same routine. 'Even the bums have money for drugs. Where do they get it?'

Deitsch spent the night in the train station, dozing and watching the train station people live, watching his new world unfold its dark life style. The next morning Deitsch ate found food, food from the garbage cans near the restaurants. He watched the experienced survivors of his new world and did what they did. He found an old sweater in a garbage can. He watched his new colleagues steal wallets from the travelers in the station. He decided to take a try at it. A woman was boarding a train. He stood close behind her with a newspaper in his hand. The woman had a handbag slung over her shoulder. Sol stood close to her and covered the handbag with the newspaper. Under the newspaper he opened the handbag and reached in and took out her wallet. He boarded the train behind her, went into the next car and then exited the train with her wallet. He had watched another bum do it and it worked. He learned other tricks. Once, as he was exiting the train, he saw a small suitcase on the rack next to the exit door. He picked it up and exited with it. Deitsch began to build confidence in himself. He began to believe that he would survive. He put the money he had collected in his shoe. He had almost 500 Reichsmarks saved up.

One morning Deitsch was awakened by someone who was taking the money from his shoe. The man took the money and ran out of the station. Deitsch got a good look at him. The thief was a large man with black hair and was wearing a checkered shirt. Deitsch saw him disappear into the subway. "I'll kill you, you son of a bitch. I'll find you and kill you."

Deitsch put his shoe back on. The bums who were awake looked at him, watched him stare into space, into the furnace of hate which had become his home, his only home. The next morning around three, the short square man showed up with his little envelopes. Sol went over to him. The square man looked at Sol and smiled.

"What do you need?"

"I don't use anything. I don't do drugs."

"What do you mean? I don't know anything about drugs. I don't understand. What are you talking about?"

"I'm not a cop. I want to work for you."

"You want to meet somebody?"

"Yes, that's right. I want to meet somebody."

"The Red Shoe in Sankt Pauli, eight in the evening."

Deitsch turned around and walked outside the train station into the world of people who don't sleep very much.

That night, Deitsch found The Red Shoe, He showed up at 8 o'clock. The Red Shoe was a bordello. Sol was greeted at the door by a black woman wearing a blonde wig. She was wearing shorts which displayed her business credentials. She escorted Sol to a bar.

"Champagne?"

"I'm looking for a man, a short man with black hair."

"That would be me."

Deitsch turned around. The short square man moved up behind Deitsch.

"Do you have anything?"

"No. I want to work for you."

"Doing what?"

"You tell me."

"You want a beer?"

"I don't drink."

"I haven't seen you around. Where you from?"

"I've lived in Hamburg all my life."

"Why didn't I see you before?"

"I lived another life before. Business man."

The man looked at Deitsch, evaluated him.

"I'm Micky."

"My name is Solomon Deitsch."

"You want to do business with me. What business did you do?"

"Women's wear. I owned a boutique."

"Boutique."

"I want to get into business again."

"How long ago was this? When were you in business?"

"I'm not sure. I think two weeks ago, two, three weeks."

"What's the address? Your old store? Maybe I'll go by, see if anything's left. You want a drink?"

"I don't drink, but have one for yourself if you want."

Micky called the bartender over.

"What we got in the kitchen? Fix my friend something, and I'll take a beer. What's the address?"

Deitsch told him the address of his boutique. Micky made a mental note of the address.

"Come by tomorrow night."

Micky drank his beer and went over to a young woman. He talked with her, but Deitsch couldn't hear what they were saying. The bartender brought Deitsch a wurst and potato salad.

"You want something to drink?"

Deitsch looked at his plate, then he looked at the bartender.

"Tea, tea with a slice lemon."

The bartender brought Deitsch a glass of hot water with a tea bag in it and a slice of lemon. Deitsch squeezed the lemon juice into the tea and added sugar. He took the glass of tea and held it in his dirty swollen hands. He felt the warmth in his palms and thought of Sadie.

Deitsch finished his meal. He left The Red Shoe and walked around the streets of Sankt Pauli. It was about 10:00 o'clock and the nightlife hadn't begun. There were some tourists walking around, a few bashful teenagers hiding their sexual urge behind loud, stupid laughing and group drunkenness. The streetwalkers were warming up for the night. There were a few customers to be had. Sol walked through the area like a businessman appraising the new season, calculating potential profits. There was some drug action. Pimps were passing out little envelopes to their young hookers. It was cold. No one was interested in standing around. Whatever they did, they did inside. Around midnight, Deitsch decided to get back to the train station. He headed toward the subway. A man came out of a bar near the subway. He was wearing a black leather jacket. Under the jacket he was wearing a checkered shirt. It was the thief who stole the money Deitsch had stolen. Deitsch followed him. The man walked down the street as if he were doing some errands. He went into a bar. Deitsch waited outside. A few minutes later the man came out and moved on down the street. Sol stayed close behind him. He looked at the man's back. He was a large man, almost six feet tall. He turned a corner and walked toward a construction site. There were no streetlights near the site. There was about 30 meters of shadow between the lighted areas. The man walked into the shadow. Deitsch picked up a large rock which was lying around near the site and followed him. When the man was about five meters into the shadow, Deitsch started running toward the man. The man turned around and Deitsch leaped up and put his legs around the man's waist and began hitting him in the face with the rock. Deitsch continued hitting him as they fell to the ground, pounding the rock into the man's face. The rock fell out of Deitsch's hand. Deitsch continued hitting the man with his fist until he had to stop to get his breath. The man didn't move. Deitsch crawled off the man's body and sat next to it. It was dark. He saw people moving in the streeet lights outside the construction area. Deitsch quickly went through the man's pockets. He found a small handgun. Deitsch put the gun in his pants pocket. He took the man's wallet and his watch, and then he walked back into the light. His hands and sleeves were covered with blood. People on the street stared at him. He looked away. He had the man's wallet in his wet bloody hand. He stuffed it into his pocket without looking in it. He went back to the subway. He stood on the platform and waited for the train. People on the platform stared at him. When the train came he got on. Suddenly he saw his reflection in the window of the door. His face was covered with blood. He tried to wipe his face. The blood had a sweet smell. He tried to wipe it away with his sweater. He got out at the train station and went into the men's room and washed his face. He took off his sweater and washed his hands and face. He threw the sweater in a garbage can near the sinks. He went into a toilet booth and took out the wallet. It was black smooth leather. It contained over a thousand Reichsmarks. There was a picture of its previous owner in it, not a bad-looking man, probably dead now. Best get rid of it, throw away everything but the money. The watch was good, big gold watch, keep that. The gun was interesting. It was heavy for something so small, black metal, who knows? Deitsch put the watch on and put the money and the gun in his pocket. He walked out of the rest room and out of the train station. He wouldn't sleep in the train station that night. He would never sleep in a train station again.

Deitsch slept in a cheap hotel near the station, one that didn't ask for identity papers. It had a bed and a bathroom with a shower. Deitsch took a long hot shower. The heat from the water and from the radiator reminded him of his former life. He looked into the full-length mirror in the room, looked at his naked body. He was thinner. He would shave tomorrow. Tomorrow he would buy a razor and some soap and shave and buy some new clothes, a new suit, a cheap new suit. He would reclaim some pieces of his old life. Where was Sadie? He wanted to tell her what happened, the things that had happened. Should he tell her that he had killed a man? Should he tell her that he was going into the drug business? He could tell her that he had lost weight. She was in a prison. At least she had food and was warm. He mainly wanted to tell her that he was grateful for what she did, not giving the police any information, not telling any lies to save her from being put in prison. He wanted to say that he loved her. If he ever saw her again, he would say that he would always love her. If they met in another life, he would love her and take care of her. Suddenly Deitsch wept. Sobs broke from his chest and he wept until he fell asleep.

The next morning Deitsch woke up in his hotel bed. It was almost three o'clock in the afternoon. He got up and went to the desk and paid for a week in advance. Then he went out and found a store that sold cheap clothes. He bought a suit and two shirts and a tie and some new underwear and some socks. He bought a winter overcoat. Then he went to a store that sold razors and soap and toothpaste and a toothbrush. He came back to the hotel. He shaved and put on his new clothes. He went out into the winter streets. He looked at his heavy gold watch. It was almost seven. He found a cheap restaurant and had some barley soup with black bread and roast chicken and tea. Then he went to The Red Shoe.

Deitsch sat at the bar. The bartender came over.

"What'll it be?"

"Tea, please, with lemon."

Micky came over to the bar.

"Hey Soli, you cleaned up. Didn't know who you were for a minute."

"Mr. Mick."

"Micky. Soli, I want to have a little talk with you. You want to come with me?"

Micky led Deitsch to a table in the back of the room. Deitsch brought his tea with him. They sat down.

"You want something to eat? You hungry?"

"Thanks, Micky, I ate already."

"It's good you cleaned up. You look different."

"What do you mean, I look different?"

"I mean last night. They're looking for a bum, not a businessman."

"You know about last night?"

"Some people saw a bum in the subway. I know about everything that goes on around here. It's OK. The guy was a fuck off."

"Who's they? Is somebody looking for me?"

"Forget it. I was over to your former business. It's under new management. Got a sign, UNDER NEW MANAGEMENT."

Deitsch listened. The store was like a family member, a family member that had been kidnapped. He remembered the office where he and Sadie had worked late at night to get everything done, get the place on its feet. The idea that other people were in his office brought rage to his mind.

"Who is this new management? What's their name? Did you see any names?"

"The sign just said UNDER NEW MANAGEMENT."

"I know who they are, the new management."

"So, talk to me, Soli. What's on your mind".

"I know the store, Micky, where everything is, the alarm, the safe."

"You think they got the same safe, the one you had?"

"I think so. The insurance company knows the combination. The 'new management' could get the combination from them. They don't expect any trouble from me. Why change the safe? The time of year is good. Christmas sales, January sales. There was a lot of money in that safe when they picked me up."

Micky looked at Deitsch.

"This country's going to hell, Soli, and everybody with it. Now it's the Jews. Tomorrow it's going to be everybody. Nobody gets away. This fucking asshole, this Hitler's going to ruin it for everybody. If it was up to me, he would be history a long time ago."

"I'm a businessman, Micky. What's your deal?"

"You give me the information. We clean the assholes out. No alarm, we take our time. The money, the stock, the works. You get 20%."

"Micky, are you going with the people who will do the job?"

"Right. I'll be there with them. That's how I work. I'll take a few guys and we'll do the job."

"Micky, I want to be there. I want to come with you."

"Be my guest. Let's talk details."

Deitsch gave Micky a complete description of the physical layout of the store, where the alarm was located, how to disarm it, where the stock was located, where the safe was, even where the toilet was. They would do the job the following week.

It was strange being in his old office at three in the morning. The pictures were gone, the pictures of him and Sadie, the wedding pictures. They had taken them away, thrown them away, probably in the garbage. Seven men were systematically cleaning out his old store. They were taking everything that wasn't nailed down, the stock, fixtures, everything that might bring in some money. Deitsch thought that the only thing that was of real value wasn't there, the wedding pictures.

Deitsch and Sadie had been cautious. They saw the way things were going in Germany and had put most of their earnings in the safe instead of depositing them in the bank. They had over three hundred thousand Reichsmarks in cash in the safe, plus several thousand in bank notes and bonds. That, plus the money from the stock, when sold on the black market, would amount to a substantial sum. Deitsch's 20% would make him a rich man in spite of the losses he had suffered from the

Government's theft. Micky's men were experienced and efficient. They knew what they were doing. In a couple of hours the place was cleaned out. Everything was put in a truck which was parked in the back of the store. After the job was done, Deitsch and Micky went to The Red Shoe. They sat at the table in the back.

"Soli, you sure you don't want a drink?"

"Just some tea. Micky, tell me about drugs. Maybe I can help you there. I'm a businessman."

"Not tonight, Soli. Don't move too fast. People notice when you move too fast. That's just what you don't want, to be noticed. You want a little fun tonight? I'll deduct it from your 20%."

"I have a wife, Micky. She's in prison somewhere. Do you know anybody?"

"You don't want to get too noticed, ask too many questions. That's business. You're a businessman. That's business."

"Micky, there's a way to do anything. If you can find out something, I would be grateful."

"Soli, you got balls. That I got to say. You got balls. I'll listen. If I hear something, I'll tell you."

Deitsch finished his tea and took a taxi back to his hotel.

Deitsch learned how the drug business worked. People brought the drugs to The Red Shoe, and Micky put them on the street. Everybody got their cut and that was it, simple. There were expenses, as with any business, and there were greedy people, as with any business. There was the question of product quality, and the secret to any business was the same, returning customers. Deitsch was fascinated with the names of his new line of goods, 'horse', 'white powder', 'Gold Dust', and there was the secondary line of goods, variations of amphetamines, 'uppers', 'downers', but the pure and simple magic word was heroin. With heroin, you had a guarantee of returning customers, as long as they stayed alive, and as long as you stayed alive. There was no real danger with the professional participants in this drug world. It was in everybody's interest that everything went smoothly. The problems occurred when a user got strung out. People on drugs are unpredictable and can be violent.

One morning, if one could call three am. morning, Deitsch and Micky were sitting at a table in The Red Shoe. Micky was drinking Scotch, and Deitsch tea.

"Soli, you want to come with me. I got to make the rounds. Do some business. You want to come?"

"Yes."

"Soli, this is not a boutique where we're going."

"I want to see how the business works, Micky."

They first went to the train station. Deitsch hadn't been there in a while. He recognized a few people. He looked at his sleeping place, where he had made his home. He felt it was his, his property, his in a way that no other place in the world was his, a place he could go to but never would again, but who knows? He only looked at it once or twice, then he got down to business and watched Micky operate.

Everything was friendly. There was this friendliness, people involved in casual friendly desperation. The business was done. People took note of Deitsch, saw that he was part of the deal, included him in their circle, their family. Family is perhaps the right word for the whole thing, the event of drugs and the way of life that everyone was participating in. The whole drug culture was the substitution for a family that had failed in everyone's life and was found in these dirty crevices, these secret corners that come to life in the early morning. Then Micky and Deitsch went to the docks.

The docks was hard-core. It was cold. Yellow night-lights mixed with mist and fog illuminated long stretches of empty streets. Huge trucks which had traveled from all parts of Europe, Poland, Russia, France, Italy were parked between the warehouses and the docks. Truck drivers slept, ate and fucked in the cabins of their mobile monsters, and some of them were waiting for Micky to come and give them their dream until morning.
They were parked in a space between the trucks. Micky turned on the car radio, turned it up loud, too loud for them to talk with each other. He let it play for two or three minutes. Then he turned it off. He took a handgun from his jacket pocket and put it on the seat next to his thigh.
     "Micky, you hear anything about my wife?"
     "Nothing, Soli."
A man and a young girl came over to the car. Micky rolled down the window. The man was drinking beer. The man leaned down and spoke briefly with

Micky, took the drugs, gave Micky some money, and he and the young girl walked away. Sol nodded to the gun next to Micky.

"Do you ever use that?"

"It's good to have."

"I have the one I took from that man. I don't have bullets for it."

"You got it with you?"

Deitsch took it out of his coat pocket and handed it to Micky. Micky took the weapon, looked at it and gave it back to Deitsch.

"Come by tomorrow."

"I never used a weapon before, only a rock."

"I don't like guns. It's OK outside, but like in a bar, a knife is better."

"I have no idea."

"In a bar, you put the knife up your sleeve. You let the guy get close, drop your arm down. The knife drops into your hand. You push the button. The blade pops out and you put it in the guy's gut, maybe a few times, take it out, push the button, drop the knife in your jacket pocket and leave."

"Isn't the knife bloody?"

"No, usually not."

"Does it bother you later?"

"People die, Soli. I got to take a piss."

Micky got out and went to the back of the car. Deitsch looked out the window at the huge trucks and thought of their stories, the stories each truck could tell. Deitsch heard a crack sound, like a firecracker. He looked out the back window. He didn't see Micky. He quickly got out of the car and found Micky lying on the asphalt. He saw the man that had bought the drugs walking toward him. The man raised his arm. Deitsch jumped to the side of the car. He opened the door and searched with his hands for the gun Micky had put on the seat. It was not there. The man came to the side of the car and stood near the door. He pointed his weapon at Deitsch. Deitsch fell to the floor of the car. His hand felt Micky's weapon on the floor of the car. Deitsch looked up and saw the man looking at him through the car door window. He fired Micky's gun wildly at the man's face. One of the bullets hit the man in the head. He fell. Deitsch kicked the door open and crawled out of the car. He crawled over the man's body. Deitsch stood up and fired three shots into the man's body. He heard someone running away. Deitsch went over to Micky. Micky was dead. The back of his head was gone. Deitsch got into the car and drove away.

Deitsch drove aimlessly around the city. Micky's last words kept sounding in his mind.

"People die, Soli."

"I won't die, Micky. Goddamn it. I won't die."

The sun came up and the part of the day that was supposed to be normal started. Deitsch drove back to his hotel. It was too early to check out, but he knew that he had to move. Micky's people would think that he had killed Micky and would come after him. He found an early morning coffee shop and had some coffee and a ham sandwich. When the stores opened, he bought a suitcase and went to his room and packed. He checked out of the hotel and walked the streets. He knew that he had to leave Hamburg. There was the problem with

Micky, and then there was also the problem of looking Jewish. He could be picked up at any minute. The population of Germany, people who had once been his friends and customers, had turned into a slimy, hysterical pile of rats using each other to crawl out of the sewer that had once been his Germany. Deitsch took a taxi to the docks. He found a freighter that was bound for Portugal. He had money. Deitsch made his way to Lisboa, Portugal. The man who had lived in Hamburg, the man with a wife named Sadie, the somewhat plump man with a small fashion boutique, had perished. He was survived by a scarecrow with hate burned into his face, and fear grafted onto his soul.

The tattoo was the thing that Sadie Deitch didn't understand. She had been taken to a 'waiting camp'. She wasn't sure where she actually was. The Germans took her clothes, even her underwear. They cut her hair. At first she wondered the whole time if this was a prison, a prison for criminals, but her fellow inmates weren't criminals. They were just ordinary women, some young, some older, women who had families, children. Sadie was happy that she didn't have any children. She thought she was in a prison for women who were accused of breaking a law. She worked in a factory which made rifles, but why the tattoo? The number tattooed on her arm? There were rumors of prisoners being murdered by the Germans, large numbers of people being executed, but they wouldn't bother putting a tattoo on her arm if they were going to shoot her. In time she found out where she was and what was going on. In time she found out everything, but to the end of her life she never understood why they had bothered to tattoo her.

After the war, Sadie Deitsch came back to her home in Hamburg, but it wasn't there. Sadie got off the train which had carried her home to nothing. Her beauty was gone. Her family was gone. She stood at the site of her one time address and looked at the symbol of her circumstance, a pile of memories. Well, she was alive, and that was the glorious sum of her entire possession. The Swiss Red Cross was helpful in putting people back together, both with themselves and with their loved ones. Sadie looked for Sol. So many had perished. Where could she begin her search? Every day she went to the board where notes were pinned up. It is a tribute to the spirit, the courage of people who pinned their hope on a wall, hope of finding a child, a father, anyone. The hope wall grew day to day. Sadie was uncomfortable being in Hamburg. She was uncomfortable being in Germany. It seemed natural at first to come back home, but what was 'natural' these days? She went to Palestine.

The human mind is always trying to crawl over a wall. It forgets what it is and looks to find out what it will become. That's how Sadie survived. This strange hot land was supposed to be the land of the Jews. Does it have to be so hot? Would it be a tragedy if the weather were a little more like it was in Germany? Did the food she was used to fit in this exotic climate? Many newcomers to Palestine sat in the outdoor cafés on Dizengoff in Tel Aviv and pretended they were in Vienna. And what is this kibbutz business? Show me one kibbutz in Germany or Poland.

There was the sea. Thank God, there was the sea. In the cool times of the day, Sadie walked on the beach. She regained her strength walking on the beach. How many memories were carried out to sea in those days after the war? How many new arrivals walked the shores of Palestine and let go of their pain, giving it to the infinite loving patient sea.

Sadie sat on the beach, on the sand. There were benches, but she liked the feeling of sand against her body. She sat near the coming and going of the water. What would she do with her life? Where was Sol? The figure being discussed was around six million. Was he one?

A man came from the sea. He emerged from somewhere in the sea and walked, dripping seawater, toward her. Sadie was annoyed. She needed her privacy. The man was very thin, bony. She was about to tell him to leave her in peace. Then she saw the blue number crudely tattooed on his forearm.

His voice was difficult to hear above the splashing sea and the wind.

"I saw you sitting alone, and wanted to talk to you."

Sadie heard her own voice ask,

"What do you want to say?"

"Just talk. Where are you from?"

"Germany. You?"

"Vilnius."

Sadie covered her arm, the number. The man said,

"Don't cover it."

Sadie slowly moved her hand away from her forearm. She felt naked. She murmured,

"The war."

The man nodded. Sadie said,

"Is there a subject other than the war?"

"Yes, America."

"Do you want to go to America? Do you have plans to go to America?"

"I think so."

"This is our land. Here. Palestine. We're safe here."

"There'll be a war here."

"We're back to war."

The man turned and looked out toward the sea.

"I want to go to New York. I want to see tall buildings. They call them skyscrapers, buildings that scrape the sky. I have some cousins in New York or Chicago."

"You're a little boy. What's your name?"

"Milkin, Jay Milkin."

"You sound like a little boy, Jay. A naive little boy. I'm Sadie, Sadie Deitsch... I need to be alone, Jay. Maybe another time."

"I'd like to talk with you again."

"I'm usually here in the late afternoon."

Jay Milkin walked away. Sadie watched him for a while as he got further and further away. Then she looked at the sea. The sun was going down. She murmured, "America."

In the meantime, Deitsch had found out that Lisboa was not Deitsch's town. It was too hot and too slow, and it just wasn't Jewish. He took a freighter to New York.

Fall, 1939. The United States wasn't in the war yet. It was 7 o'clock in the morning, grey and cold. New York was huge. Deitsch had a little money left, but the ocean passages had made a big dent in his wallet. Illegal operations are expensive. He had to come on to some money fast. He didn't speak English, and he didn't know anybody. He walked onto the foreign shores of the Manhattan docks and checked into a cheap hotel on 43rd and 10th Avenue, Hotel Florida. He was too excited to sleep, so he walked the streets near the hotel. It was a lively neighborhood even at that hour. Italian street vendors were hawking their fresh vegetables and fish. The sidewalks vibrated with vitality. Deitsch felt good. Something would come of this. Deitsch bought a huge sandwich and some hot coffee, which he drank from a paper coffee cup. He stood on the street and watched the people going about their morning business. Stores opened. Children went to school. What fascinated him were the black people. He had never seen so many black people. There were also cream-colored people from Puerto Rico or Cuba. The whole thing seemed to be a kind of ballet, dancers moving in a unique whirlpool without really bumping into each other. The other element which astonished him was dirt. So much garbage and dirt. It didn't seem to bother anybody that the streets were in need of repair. It didn't slow down the traffic. The traffic lights seemed to be more for decoration than for traffic control. The large sea of pedestrians moved safely across the streets as if by the grace of God. Something good would come of this.

What was it that made Deitsch feel at home in this city where he could barely speak to anybody? Yes, this was a Jewish city. Deitsch was far from holy. He was unholy. He had tasted killing. Not Cain's killing, Satan's killing. Yet he felt he had to find the Jewish ghetto in this hodgepodge of human babble. He found the Lower East Side. Here were the Poles and Russians, the Jews from before his time, and in his time and after his time. Here he found himself. He felt spread out over time, over centuries. Here were the peddlers who left their survival recipes in his blood. He could walk among them, eat among them, walk past synagogues, watch the religious go about their chosen steps, their ancient dance. Here he was safe from the slaughter he knew was going on in Europe.

There was a bar on the lower East Side, between 7th and Avenue B, right next to Tompkins Square Park. It was a European family bar. There were cold cuts and slices of tomatoes and onions on the bar. They were free. You drank your stein of beer and maybe had a pickled hard-boiled egg and helped yourself to the side dishes. Children came running in and out, checking with their parents who were sitting at wooden tables drinking with friends from the neighborhood. Deitsch wandered in and sat at the bar. The bartender came over. Deitsch's face was new to him, but his face type was well known.

"What will you have?"
Deitsch said one of the few words he knew in English.

"Beer, a beer."

Deitsch was given a stein of cold beer. It was a rare occasion that Deitsch drank anything other than tea. It was a sign that he was beginning to feel safe. He heard people conversing in English and Polish. At one booth a young woman was talking with a heavy-set man. The woman's eyes were blue, very blue. Her hair was yellow. Deitsch watched her. She seemed like a beautiful, vulgar child. He couldn't see her lower body. Her arms and breasts were full. Sex and calculated helplessness poured out of her. The man she was talking with didn't have the look of a suitor. He looked like a kind friend who had been in a lot of fights. His arms were strong, and his eyes looked like he had been hit in the face a lot. There was one other thing. They were speaking a mixture of English and Yiddish. The young woman's face was furious.

"Er will zehn toisunt dollars, der mumzer. He wants ten thousand dollars, the bum."

"Er ist meshugge. He's crazy." The man tried to cool her down.

"I'm afraid of this shmuck. Fucking wop shmuck."

"Sandy, if I had it, I'd give it to you."

"No, Lew, if I had it, if I gave him 10, he'd want 20. There's no way with this dreck. Ich chob em in drerd. He can go to hell."

Deitsch was intrigued with this woman. He wanted to help her. Who was threatening her? He spoke in Yiddish.

"Excuse me. I just got here in New York, just a few days. I'm here just a few days."

Lew looked at Deitsch.

"Where do you come from?"

159

"Germany. Are you born here?"

"Lithuania. I was born in Lithuania, near Vilnius."

"That's Poland now."

"Poland, Lithuania, big deal."

Sandy saw possibilities.

"Are you here on business?"

"I'm looking to start a business."

'Start a business' means money, she thought.

"What business are you in?"

"I am in women's apparel."

Sandy smiled.

"Do you have family here?"

"No."

"Sandy Sandinsky." She gave Deitsch her hand.

"Deitsch, Solomon Deitsch." He took her hand. He noticed that her arm was bruised. Lew extended his hand. It was a boxer's hand, massive and in Lew's case, gentle.

"Lew Brown. Have a seat."

"Thank you. It's good to speak to someone." Sandy was sizing the newcomer up, slim man, good-looking, crazy eyes, acquainted with money. Sandy was drinking beer. Lew, orange juice. Lew spoke with a gentle voice.

"Things are getting rough in Europe. That's what I hear. For Jews it's getting rough."

Deitsch looked at Sandy. He saw Sadie.

"Forget Europe. We are here. Sandy, I am a businessman. I speak frankly. I overheard your talking with Mr. Brown. I will help you."

Sandy was completely thrown.

"Mr. Deitsch, I don't understand."

"You are in some sort of mess. Maybe I can help you."

"I don't know what to say. I have some problems with someone, but I can't get a perfect stranger involved. These people, this person is, well, they are not nice people. It's a man that I work for."

"What does he want?"

"He wants me to continue to work for him."

"You don't want to work there anymore?"

"Mr. Deitsch…"

"Sol."

"Sol… I thank you, but this is not a simple thing."

"Let's make it simple."

Lew spoke gently.

"Sol, this is a private affair."

Deitsch's eyes began to move back and forth, first to Sandy then back to Lew.

"Excuse me. I'm looking for an apartment in this neighborhood. Do you know about an apartment around here?"

Lew was happy to change the subject.

"6th and Avenue B. Near the corner. There will be a place free. A friend is going to California in a few weeks. He's looking for someone to take over his place so he doesn't have trouble with the landlord about the rent contract."

"That sounds good."

"I'll take you over there. Are you free later?"

"When, when do you want to go?"

"We can meet here around seven."

Deitsch touched Sandy's arm.

"If I can help you, let me know." He stood up.

"See you at seven."

He left. Sandy watched him go.

"Who is this guy?"

Lew smiled.

"I don't know, but I think we'll find out."

The apartment was a railroad apartment, living room, dining room, kitchen, bedroom all in a row. It was fine for Deitsch, cheap and in a neighborhood he felt good in. It was near an area called Little Italy. The area fascinated Deitsch. Italian immigrants, families from 'the old country' filled the streets with a simple vitality, good cheap restaurants, children playing in the streets, a game called stick ball, a version of American baseball. Men stood around and smoked cigarettes and Italian cigars, little dark cigars called 'stogies'. Most of the people were poor, but there was money in the Italian neighborhood. Black limousines were parked in front of restaurants and so-called 'social clubs'. Deitsch didn't know how things worked, but he was keeping his eyes open. There seemed to be no crime in the area, no streetwalkers, no drugs. It was a family atmosphere.

It was three in the morning. Deitsch was sleeping. There was a knock at the door. Deitsch woke up and put on his pants. He went to the door.

"It's Sandy."

Deitsch opened the door. Sandy was standing in a raincoat. Her face was swollen. She had a black eye.

"Can I come in?"

"Come in."

Sandy came in and sat down on the sofa in the living room. Deitsch went to the bedroom and put on a shirt. He came back to the living room.

"You want some tea or some coffee?"

"No thanks. You said you would help me."

"What happened?"

"This shmuck I work for, I'm one of his girls."

"Go on."

"I have clients, men clients."

"I understand."

"I want out. It would cost me money to get out, to buy out."

"Why don't you just quit?"

"He would find me. He said he would find me."

"How much money?"

"He said ten thousand, but he'll want more."

"Stay here until your face is OK. I'll sleep on the couch. In a few days everything will be OK."

"Sol, I didn't know what to do."

"We'll talk tomorrow."

Deitsch brought Sandy to the bedroom. He took a blanket back to the living room and slept on the couch.

The next morning Sandy's face looked like hell. They drank coffee.

"Sol, I don't know how to thank you. I don't want you to get mixed up with this shit."

"It will be over in a few days. You stay here. Call Lew, tell him where you are. No one else. What do you like to eat?"

"Sol, you don't know me. This could be dangerous. This son of a bitch is connected. Mafia, you know what I'm talking about?"

"I don't exist in this country, Sandy. No papers, nothing. I just stepped off a boat, and that's it. I'm invisible. No one can find me. I had to leave Europe, not just because I'm Jewish. You're safe here. I'll take care of this man."

"He'll want money. He'll drain you dry."

"I'll take care of him. How do you operate? Hotel, what?"

"I work in a hotel, work the bar. Actually, I sing opera. That's what I'm studying to do, be an opera singer. I got into this shit to make some money to study. My teacher says I got a good voice."

"Opera singer?"

"Yeah, this Italian fuck said he would help me."

"Just stay put a few days. Next week we'll take care of everything. I'll talk to him."

A few days later Deitsch checked into the hotel where Sandy worked from. It was a middle price hotel in the West Fifties. It was about one in the morning. Deitsch and Sandy were in the hotel room.

"OK, Sandy, you call this man up. Tell him you're with a client, a dealer from Lisboa, Portugal. Tell him I want to take you back to Portugal, and I want to deal some drugs. Tell him to bring something, and that I want to make a deal to take you to Portugal. Tell him I have money, he is to come to the hotel."

"Sol, what the hell are you going to do?"

164

"Just call him."

Sandy took the hotel phone and placed the call.

"Carlo, this is Sandy. Look… wait… look. I've been sick. Yeah, I know… I was at a friend's … yeah. Look, Carlo, I'm at the hotel… right. I'm with a client… yeah. He wants to talk with you. He's from Portugal. Look, he wants me to go back to Portugal with him… I know, I told him. He says he wants to give you the money… right. He says he's got the cash, and he wants to take me back. Right. With him to Lisboa, someplace … right. He says he wants to deal, wants you to come here to the hotel and work out a deal. He says bring some stuff with you."

Sandy hands the receiver to Sol.

"He wants to talk to you."

"Tell him I don't talk on the phone."

Sandy speaks into the receiver.

"He don't talk on the phone. That's what he said, he don't talk on the phone. It's no bullshit, Carlo. I'm tellin' ya. It's no bullshit. OK. Room 643. OK. Right." Sandy hangs up the receiver.

"He's coming."

Deitsch and Sandy waited. Deitsch took off his suit jacket. Sandy lay down on the bed and smoked. It was a long twenty minutes. There was a knock at the room door. Sandy went to the door.

"Carlo?"

"Yeah."

She opened the door. A Mediterranean-looking man walked past her and into the room, medium height, actually tall for an Italian. Sol was sitting in a chair in his shirtsleeves. He smiled at Carlo. He stood up.

Deitsch was a head shorter than Carlo. Perfect. Carlo spoke to him.

"You want to talk or what."

Sandy spoke from behind Carlo.

"He don't speak English too good."

"What the fuck does he speak?"

"German."

"I thought you said he came from Portugal."

"He gets around."

Deitsch stood smiling at Carlo. Carlo smiled back.

"So you're a kraut. You bastards are doing the right thing in Krautland, getting rid of the Yids."

Deitsch continued to smile. He remembered Micky's instructions. The knife was in his shirt sleeve. He took a step toward Carlo as if he were going to shake his hand. Then he put his arm down and the knife fell into his palm. He pushed the button and the blade sprang out. Deitsch plunged it into Carlo's stomach using an upward motion. Carlo grabbed his stomach. His jaw dropped. Deitsch took the knife in his hand and began plunging it into Carlo's chest, again and again. Carlo fell to the floor. Deitsch stood over him. "Heil Hitler."

Deitsch cleaned out Carlo's pockets. He and Sandy left the room. Micky had been wrong about the blood.

Deitsch and Sandy went back to his place on the Lower East Side. Carlo had about eight hundred dollars in his pocket. He had it in his pants pocket, not in his billfold. He also had some pills and other drugs, probably amphetamines, in his jacket.

Deitsch wasn't familiar with the drugs. Sandy gave him a rundown on what they were. They were worth about a thousand dollars on the street. The question was where to unload them. Deitsch thought the harbor might be a good spot. Deitsch was cautious.

"We're going to have to be quiet for a while. His people are going to try to get some information. He had other girls. If anybody asks you anything, you were with Lew. You have been sick, and Lew took care of you for a while. We'll talk to Lew. Later we can contact his girls and keep things going, but you're out. I'll take care of you."

"Why did you do this for me, Sol?"

"Everything doesn't have to have a reason, Sadie. Some things don't have a reason. They just happen."

"Sandy."

"What?"

"You said, 'Sadie'."

"Sandy, some things happen that don't have a reason."

Deitsch took care of Sandy, took care of her voice lessons, acting lessons. Eventually he got her an apartment on the Upper West Side. They spent evenings together, but it wasn't in payment for favors, nor was it a love affair. As Deitsch put it, some things don't need reasons. Sandy helped Deitsch build up his business. She introduced him to Abe, the porno man, helped him with drug suppliers. She knew the doctors who were heavy on needs and low on scruples. In a few short years, Deitsch built up his business. The thought of becoming a legitimate businessman never occurred to him. Crime was like a drug which numbed his mind to things he didn't want to remember. He took Micky's advice, 'Don't move too fast'. Deitsch moved very cautiously, covering every possibility, thinking through every move a thousand times. He moved into drugs and prostitution. He made money and used money as a weapon to buy more control and to buy people who would ensure that control. He built a reputation as someone who would be very generous if you worked with him. He would be generous and fair. On the other hand, he went a little insane if he thought someone betrayed him. His was a simple formula: work with me and you will get rich, work against me and you will end up dead. He felt that his life was a continuing struggle to protect himself from one form of evil or another, evil which was bent on destroying him, a curse which had followed him around the world, taking everything from him and leaving him to begin again and again. Sol Deitsch had one goal in life: to survive.

Sandy was grateful to Deitsch. Over the years, he was generous to her, granting her every whim, as if she were the family he had lost during the war. She was his daughter that he never had, his lover and wife. She was loyal to him. She knew that if he felt the slightest doubt about her loyalty to him, his insane terror of being destroyed again would put her life in danger. This thing with Max and Chrystal, she wanted to help them, but she had to be careful.

"Sol, I don't think Max, or anyone in his right mind, would put you in a compromising position. Anyway, he came to me and asked me to reassure you that you have nothing to worry about."

"Why did he come to you? Why not to me?"

"Sol, he doesn't even know who you are. He doesn't even know your name. He can't say anything that would implicate you."

"He knows Abe's name. If Abe goes, I go. I set Abe up in business, just like I set you up. Only Abe's business is different from yours. You're legit. Nothing can happen to you. Abe's a different story. This Max is either with the program or he's out. Hey, Sandy, who's gonna take care of you if I get put away? If I lose, you lose, everybody loses. I can't take the chance."

"I appreciate that, Sol. I know that the cops questioned him, and he gave them nothing. I know that."

"I know that too. But they questioned him down at the precinct. That's not the same thing as being on the stand. Not the same thing at all."

Sandy knew that she was not getting anywhere with Deitsch. What he was saying made sense from his point of view. His argument was rational. But it wasn't really important what Deitsch said; it was how he looked at you that made the difference, how his eyes looked. Deitsch's eyes burned into her, looking for some indication of either loyalty or betrayal. If for any reason he felt he couldn't count on her completely to support any action Deitsch would take, then Sandy was in serious danger. To make his point, Deitsch explained why Lewis Brown had been a risk.

"That was the problem with Lew, Sandy. You can't take any risks. Lew was hit in the head

169

too many times. Put him on the stand, and he wouldn't know what was going on. A doctor gave me something. He didn't feel nothing. I sent him a couple of little beauties, young. He had a good time. I had no choice, Sadie."

When Deitsch started using his wife's name, then Sandy knew it was time to drop the subject.

"I understand, Sol. Forget it. You're right. You can't take any chances."

Christmas came and went. Other than the blue steel weapon, there were no extraordinary presents exchanged. If Christmas is an addiction, then this year Max and Chrystal were clean. They were intensely involved in what's known as everyday life, and everyday life was La Traviata. The whole adventure, working in New York, being part of the New York theatre scene, was a good feeling. It was as if another part of the life puzzle was coming into place. The Abe and 'Sandy's friend' business just didn't fit into their idea of who they were. Their life was theater and each other.

Deitsch, on the other hand, was coming apart. Subpoenas were being issued to prospective witnesses for the State. While he had always been careful, Abe had been sloppy. Abe had handled his business dealings more like a Bacchus who lived from whim to whim, rather than a criminal who had to cover his tracks and make sure that no money transactions could be traced back to him. Deitsch couldn't simply liquidate every potential danger. His fight to survive would take place in court, not on the street. Deitsch did have one advantage. Most of the characters Abe had worked with had criminal records. Deitsch's lawyers could easily show that testimony given by these witnesses was unreliable. One potential witness, however, didn't have a record. In fact this potential witness was an upstanding member of the theater community, a completely credible witness. This potential witness was Max Fagan. If he were to be called to the stand, Max could divulge information which would make the case for the State. Deitsch's choice was simple.

When a production moves from the rehearsal rooms to the main stage, a kind of quantum leap takes place in the soul. Chrystal looked out into the four thousand-seat house which she and her colleagues would have to fill with their voices and their presence. Chrystal was surprised to realize that instead of frightening her or making her feel insignificant, the enormous auditorium made her feel free. She could breathe and move and sing freely, more freely than in a large room and certainly more freely than in a studio. This magic place was, in a strange way, safe. People could watch her and listen to her, but no one could touch her. Only her colleagues would be close to her, colleagues she had grown to love and trust. For Chrystal, the stage was what Nature had intended when, in the beginning, God created.

Max had arranged for Sam Levine to work on the production as part of the assistant production staff. Max was aware that Sam was undergoing a decision process. Why give up access to the colorful world which Abe and his cast of characters provided. It was fun to have entrée to smoky dens of mystery. Who knows? Maybe he could use this experience in some future role he would play. And there was, of course, the money. On the other hand, Sam would do nothing to comprise Max. The problem was solved one afternoon, when Max got a phone call. They were in the middle of a rehearsal. Sam took the call.

"Mr. Fagan is busy at the moment. Can I take a message?" It was Jose. "I need to speak to Max. Tell him its Jose."

Sam quietly went over to Max and whispered.

"A guy named Jose wants to talk to you."

Max was startled. Why in the hell would Jose call in the middle of the day?

"You guys continue. I'll be right back."

Max went to the production office and took the call.

"Hello, Jose. What's up?"

"Max, Abe is dead. You don't have to worry about him anymore. Sandy's friend is covering all his bases, and I think you better keep your eyes open."

"What did he die of?"

"One of those famous heart attacks."

"Thanks, Jose. I'll call you later. Wait, you don't have a phone. Call me tonight. Is that OK?"

"Around eight?"

"Good. Talk to you later."

Max walked slowly back to the rehearsal. Chrystal was rehearsing the scene with her lover's father. When the scene was over, Max stopped the rehearsal.

"Thirty minutes. It's really going great. Take a break. We'll start with Alfredo's re-entrance. Chrystal, I got some good news. Sammy, it's something for you too."

The three of them talked quietly in the middle of the dimly-lit auditorium.

"I just got a call from Jose. Abe is dead. Heart attack."

Chrystal was dubious.

"Is that good news?"

Max explained.

"I think so. Abe was the only one who knew all about Sandy's friend. With him gone, this asshole should begin to relax. You see what I mean with these guys, Sam. It's not a movie. It's good that you got out. Where these guys are going, you don't want to go."

Sam was stunned.

"I can't believe what's happening. Abe, that big fat guy. I can't believe he was murdered. Maybe he really did have a heart attack. God knows he was fat enough. Do you think it was murder? Is that what you're saying, Max?"

"That's what I'm saying, Sam."

"Is that what this guy Jose thinks?"

"Sammy, you and me and Chrystal, we're theater people. We portray gangsters. We can even think like them to some degree, but when the shit hits the fan, they can do things that we can't do. To not understand that fact can get you in a lot of trouble, even get you killed."

Chrystal was worried.

"Are you in danger again, my love? Is this shit happening
again?"

"We're OK. I'm not connected to that world. We're OK."

Chrystal wasn't convinced.

Sandy had never seen Deitsch be so nervous.

"I'm trying to restore what I had in the old days, Sandy. Not just for me, but for us both. They took it all away, but I'll get it back."

"I believe you, Sol. You'll do it."

"Sadie, I've got to get that kid, that Max. He can screw everything up. You understand, Sadie. I don't like it. I know about the kid. Married and all that, but he is just at the wrong place at the wrong time, just like we were at the wrong place at the wrong time. We didn't do nothing to deserve what happened to us. Just the wrong place at the wrong time." His eyes burned into her.

"You understand?"

"I understand, Sol. You have to do what you have to do."

"You're the only one who stands by me, just like you did then. You didn't tell them nothing. You stood by me, and I'm going to make it up to you. You want a dress shop? Like in the old days? Anything you want, it's yours. I love you, Sadie, I always loved you. Nobody took that away. But this guy's got to go."

"Sol, you do what you think is right. You understand these things. I don't, but you do. Sol, I got to go to the studio for a while, just a short while, got to get some papers I want you to look at. I'll bring them here, be right back. If you want, I'll stay here tonight."

"What kind of papers?"

"Some tax stuff I don't understand. Can you help me with this? You know me and figures."

174

"You was always good at figures, better than me. You always did the bills and stuff."

"Yeah, but this is something I don't understand. You can show me. Something with last year's electric bills. They don't make sense."

"Sure, Sandy, bring 'em over. I'll see if I can help you out."

"I'll be right back, sweetheart. Fix yourself a drink, but leave some for me."

She kissed Deitsch's forehead. "I'll be right back." Sandy went out the door and into the hall. Deitsch waited until he heard the elevator take her down. Then he followed. Sandy caught a cab to her fitness studio. She ran upstairs to her office and dialed Max's number.

Max and Chrystal were in their apartment, waiting for Jose's call. It was almost eight o'clock. The phone rang. Max answered.

"Jose?"

" Max? This is Sandy, Sandy, Max."

"Sandy! I was expecting another call. Sandy, what's up?"

"Max, listen, I don't have much time. Max, it's my friend. Max, your life is in danger. He's going to kill you, Max. He's going to kill you. Max... ."

"Sandy? Sandy? Hello? Hello? Sandy?" Max puts the phone down.

"It was Sandy. Some problem with the connection. The line went dead."

"What did she want?"

"I don't know, something about her friend. She'll call back."

The phone rang again. Max quickly picked it up.

"Sandy, is that you?"

"It's Jose. Max, listen. This guy's going bananas. He's liable to do anything. You got that gun that Chrystal's weapon license let you buy? Did you get the gun?"

"Yeah, Jose, we got it. What the hell is going on?"

"This fucking nut has lost it. Lots of subpoenas being issued. He's lookin' to kill anybody who might have any connection to him. You guys got to be very careful. Get the hell out of town till this blows over. Go somewhere, anywhere, just disappear a while."

"We got a show that's opening next week, Jose. We're not going anywhere. If this bastard shows up, I'll blow his fucking brains out."

"You don't know how he will come at you, or he might have someone else do it. You don't even know what he looks like. You're fucking sitting ducks. Do you guys want to come uptown, stay up here for a while? I can arrange something."

"I'll talk it over with Chrystal."

"Don't talk too long. The guy's a nut. Max, take care of the little woman and yourself. If you need anything, I'll give you a number you can call. Anytime, day or night. They will get to me. Max, I love you guys."

"We know, Jose. We love you too."

"Take care."

Click.

"Jose, thanks."

He had already hung up.

Max put the receiver back on the hook.

"Darlin', we got a problem. Jose thinks this screwball will try something. You'll be standing there in front of four thousand people. One of them might be this fuck face. What do you need? We can postpone the premiere till things cool down, tell 'em you're sick. I don't think we should take any unnecessary chances."

"Max. It's you he's after, not me. What do you want to do?"

"I want to have a long life with you. Have children with you.
Maybe we should take Jose's advice and disappear a while."

"Let's sleep on it. Tomorrow we can decide. How 'bout a wee nip?"

"I want to keep a clear head. I'll drink when this is over, believe me, I will."

"Let's load the weapon. Who knows?"
They took out the blue steel weapon from the night table and put the serious-looking ammunition in the chamber. Then they held each other until sleep finally gave them rest.

The theatre became a bastion of safety for Max and Chrystal. There was the guard at the backstage entrance. Of course, an enterprising person could sneak into the theatre, but in general everybody knew everybody or knew everybody's face, and a new face would stand out. Max and Chrystal felt a load fall off their shoulders when they were safely inside the theatre. The tech rehearsal was scheduled to begin at six o'clock. Chrystal and the other singers could take it easy tonight and mark, rest their voices. The main emphasis would be on the technical considerations. Both Chrystal and Max were exhausted. The tension was beginning to show in Chrystal's voice and in Max's patience. It was toward the end of the rehearsal. The stage was full with the chorus and singers. They were adjusting the lights for the party scene. Chrystal was standing backstage, waiting to go on. One of the stagehands was reading the Free Press while waiting for the next scene change. Chrystal suddenly grabbed the paper from his hands and stared at a picture of Sandy on the front page.

EXERCISE STUDIO OWNER MURDERED!

Tears poured from her eyes.

"Sandy! Sandy!"

She walked onto the stage with the newspaper in her hands. Her face was dissolved in anguish and tears. The singers were stunned. Her colleagues ran over to her and tried to understand what was going on. Max was sitting in the auditorium watching the rehearsal from the director's desk. Chrystal walked down to the edge of the stage and held out the newspaper towards Max.

"Sandy! She's dead, Max! He killed her!!!"

She crumbled to the floor.

Max ran up to the stage and lifted Chrystal from the floor. He put his arms around her. He took the paper from her hands and read. 'Sandra Sandinsky was found shot dead this morning in her exercise studio.' No apparent motive for the killing was mentioned. Max and Chrystal put their arms around each other. Slowly the cast and chorus stepped toward the embraced couple. Some put their arms around them. Some just stood quietly. Their

unspoken message was clear. 'We're here for you.'
That's how the rehearsal ended.

Sol Deitsch was spinning in a flood of images. He
saw Sandy's face as she pleaded for her life. He
saw his wife Sadie screaming hysterically. He saw
the lawyers mocking him, shouting at him. "Jew
pig! Thief! Murderer!"
Deitsch ran from the exercise studio, out onto
Broadway. He was holding the gun he had used in
his hand. No one seemed to notice. Quickly he put
it in his pocket. His eyes burned into every face he
saw, looking to see if someone might have heard or
seen something, someone who might be a witness.
It was a cold winter evening. Everyone seemed to
be going about his business, intent on getting to
some destination out of the cold. Deitsch aimlessly
walked the streets. He was alone again. All because
of this Max. This Max Fagan. Max had forced him
to kill Sandy. He could destroy everything Deitsch
had built. Years of work wasted. He would have to
begin again. Leave New York, maybe leave
America, maybe go back to Germany. Slowly
Deitsch began to calm down. He had wandered the
streets for a few hours.

Slowly he organized his life. It was not the first
time he had had to start from scratch. He had
money. He could pack his bags. Jews did it all the
time, throughout history. He could pack his bags
and fly anywhere. He had several passports with
different names. Sandy's last advice to him had
been to have a drink. That's what he would do, go
home and have a drink. She had said 'Fix yourself a

179

drink, Sol. Leave some for me. I'll be right back.'
Good, he would go home and have a drink and wait
for her. Sadie always liked a drink in the evening.
He would go home and quietly plan the destruction
of Max Fagan.

The dress rehearsal was a tense evening. Chrystal
got through it, but she was shaking throughout the
rehearsal. There was a small invited audience in the
auditorium. Max overheard comments that they
made among themselves.

"This Miss Bergman was good last summer,
but she seems a bit over her head here in New York.
She sounds tired."

"I think the role is a bit much for her."
They were both happy when the rehearsal was over.
As they were leaving the theatre, they were met by
the two detectives who had interviewed them
several months ago.

"Mr. Fagan. Good evening. Good evening,
Miss Bergman."

"My name is Mrs. Fagan. Good evening,
gentlemen."

"We're sorry to bother you, Oh, I guess
congratulations are in order. When were you
married?"
Max informed the two men.

"Several months ago. What can we do for
you?"

"I wish I had a better wedding present. I'm
afraid I must serve you with this."
It was a subpoena to appear in court.

"Can we give you a lift somewhere?"

"That would be very nice, thank you."

They got into the police car. Max noticed the worried looks from some of the cast who were coming out of the theatre.

"Don't worry. They're just giving us a lift home. See you Sunday. Get some rest. Everything's OK."

The police car drove off.

Under the best of circumstances, the day before a premiere is hell. These were not the best of circumstances. There was one good thing: the hearing was scheduled for Thursday. Sunday was the premiere. Monday and Tuesday were off. Wednesday was the second show, so by Thursday a lot of the tension around the show would be over. At this point Max could hardly protect Sandy's 'friend', so he decided to cooperate fully with the prosecution. He just had to stay alive until Thursday.

Sol Deitsch's Saturday was a busy one. His plan was simple. He would pack some clothes along with over a million dollars in cash and bank notes in a suitcase. He would put some formal wear, tuxedo, shoes etc. in a paper bag. Then he would leave his New York apartment forever, and, wearing some old blue jeans and an old sweater, he would take a cab to Kennedy Airport. He would leave the suitcase in a locker at the airport. Using one of his phony passports, he would then purchase a plane ticket to Germany. He would return to New York and check into a small hotel in Chelsea. Sunday, he would arrive at the theatre dressed in his formal wear in time for the reception, which was scheduled after the premiere. On the way to the theatre he would dispose of the blue jeans and sweater. New York City Opera was well known for its lavish post-premiere receptions. They were formal functions. The social elite always attended. And while Max and Chrystal were celebrating the evening, he would simply walk up to them and shoot them both. Then in the confusion, he would walk out of the opera house and take a taxi to Kennedy Airport, spend the night at the airport, and the next morning he would fly to Germany. Simple.

Chrystal and Max slept late. The performance starts at eight o'clock. They would get to the theatre around six-thirty, relax, check everything. Chrystal would have time to warm up the voice, get into make-up, gather her thoughts. They had come a long way together, and, God willing, they had a long road before them. Tonight Max and Chrystal had two objectives, one, to give themselves to the moment and have a good premiere, and two, to not get shot.

The guard at the stage entrance greeted Max and Chrystal with a warm smile.

"Good evening, Mr. and Mrs Fagan. Break a leg tonight."

You're not supposed to say thanks, so they just smile and take the elevator which leads to the dressing rooms. The weapon a little bulky under Max's tuxedo jacket. Normally it would have been uncomfortable. Tonight it felt comfortable. He was not licensed to carry the weapon, but that was an unimportant detail. Max left Chrystal to get prepared for the performance, but without making it too obvious, he always remained within a short distance from her. He called Sammy over.

"Sammy, I want you in the house, in the back. I'm going to stay near Chrystal. If you see something you don't like, any goddamned thing, you come to me quick. I have no idea what this prick looks like; just keep your eyes open. Sammy, don't do anything, he's probably carrying a weapon. Maybe something will happen, maybe it won't. See you later."

Max spoke in a quiet voice. The pre-curtain speech was brief.

"There is no way that Chrystal and I can say what we feel for you. Times have been strange. They've been ugly. Alone, Chrystal and I might have broken. Because of the support you have given us, and because of the love and support we feel for you, this night will be a triumph. It will be our triumph. We love you all."

Chrystal went back to her dressing room to wait for the 'on stage' call. Max came with her.

He spoke gently.

"There's a goddess in you, my love, a goddess more powerful than anything I could imagine. I'm honored by your tenderness and your belief in me, in us. I won't be far away from you tonight, not ever. See you later."

He kissed her and left.

Chrystal was alone. She looked at herself in the mirror. There's no way to avoid this moment in theatre. No one can be with you now, now just before you go on. It's the lonely hell before some hoped-for magic will save you from oblivion.

Maybe Max was right, she thought. Maybe there is magic in me. If there is, good, if not, God help me. The voice of the stage manager interrupted her thoughts.

"Miss Bergmann, on stage."

Sol Deitsch arrived at the theatre in time for the last scene. Someone was sitting in the seat that he had bought, but that was not important to him. He found an empty seat at the back. He made himself comfortable just as the curtain opened to reveal a young woman in a nightgown. She seemed so vulnerable and alone. 'So that's Mrs. Fagan,' he thought. He remembered that Sadie loved opera. He hadn't been to an opera in many years. His mind wandered back to Hamburg, to evenings with Sadie at the theatre. He would be in Hamburg soon. America was almost just a memory now. He had money. He would build an empire just as he had always planned. This whole thing was really for the best. He would come home to his Germany in triumph. An explosion interrupted his thoughts. The opera had come to an end and the audience was wild. Chrystal's performance soared beyond anything she had ever done. When she took her bow, a wave of almost hysterical enthusiasm greeted her. She could barely hold back tears of gratitude and relief. The applause continued for almost twenty minutes. The audience wouldn't let the cast go. Finally all semblance of formality evaporated, and the cast and the production staff embraced each other and applauded the audience. Sol Deitsch sat quietly, waiting for the right moment to make his move.

The reception was royal. Tables had been arranged in the foyer, where exquisite food was being served. As the singers came into the foyer, after having gotten out of their make-up and costumes and had donned their evening attire, they were greeted with applause by the waiting guests. The artists were escorted to the different tables, where they were introduced to their public, wealthy supporters of the arts.

Max and Chrystal entered together. They were greeted with bravos and expressions of genuine enthusiasm. They were led to a table and introduced to the two couples who were to be their special guests for the evening, a Mr. and Mrs. Richard Johnson and a Mr. and Mrs. Jay Milkin. Lovely appetizers, wine and lamb chops were on the menu, but Max and Chrystal were too excited to eat. The guests rained compliments on the two new celebrities and in fact on the whole cast. Mrs. Milkin was especially moved by Chrystal. Her English had a slight European accent, perhaps German.

"When I was a young woman, I always wanted to sing opera. Times were different then, different from now."

Max was curious about her accent. Then he noticed her arm. She was wearing an elegant evening gown with long sleeves, not long enough to cover what looked like a tattoo on her left forearm. Max immediately recognized what it was, a concentration camp tattoo. She was a beautiful woman. Her face was lined with experience. Mr. Milkin had a heavy, fleshy face, dark, warm eyes. They both looked to be in their sixties.

"Yes, I wanted to sing, so you, my dear, you are a very fortunate woman to have such a gift and to be able share it with us, and we are very fortunate to be your audience."

"Thank you. I almost quit singing. Max, very subtly, talked me back into it. Having a voice is not the only lucky thing that happened to me." Chrystal gave Max a warm look. Max changed the subject.

"Mrs. Milkin, is your accent German? I think Chrystal should go to Germany. Opera is really part of everyday life in Europe." Mrs. Milkin's eyes clouded over.

"I haven't been to Germany in many years." Mrs. Johnson asked Chrystal,

"Do you have children? Are there any other music makers on the horizon?" Chrystal smiled.

"We have a friend who couldn't be here tonight, a dear friend, who won't be happy until he hears some baby sounds keeping us awake all night."

Sol Deitsch wandered through the foyer. His eyes didn't fit in with the festive atmosphere. He had a small revolver in his pocket. The kind of weapon he would use required that he be close to the victims. That was fine with him. He wanted to be close. He wanted to watch them. Deitsch was becoming impatient. There were almost a thousand people in the foyer, guests, waiters, members of the opera company. He wanted to get the thing over with, catch his taxi and be off to his new life. First he spotted Chrystal. The man next to her was very probably Max Fagan, but he wanted to be sure. There was no room for mistakes. He walked over to the table. The three couples were involved in conversation.

Deitsch glared at Max and spoke in a loud voice.

"Max Fagan?"

Max looked up.

"Yes?"

Deitsch was about to take the pistol from his pocket when Mrs. Milkin turned and looked at the strange man standing at the table. Their eyes met for the smallest fraction of a second. Deitsch quickly turned and walked away. Mrs. Milkin was briefly stunned, but she regained her composure. Mr. Milkin noticed her strange look.

"What's the matter, darling? Do you know that man?

"No. He just reminded me of someone, someone I knew in Germany."

"Maybe he was someone you knew. Do you want me to look for him?"

"The man I knew perished. The man I knew was killed. He just looks a little like him. Yes, Chrystal, may I call you Chrystal?"

"Of course, Mrs. Milkin."

"Call me Sadie. Yes, Chrystal, you should go to Germany."

The festivities wound down, and everyone left, either to continue celebrating someplace else or to go home. Max and Chrystal went home. As they left the theatre, they noticed a crowd gathered around the fountain outside the opera house. An ambulance had just pulled away, followed by a police car. Max and Chrystal were looking for a taxi. Max asked a man at the edge of the gathered crowd.

"What happened? What's all the excitement?"

"Some nut shot himself, just put a gun in his mouth and shot himself. New York. Man, never a dull moment."

Max and Chrystal walked into their apartment and kicked off their shoes and weapon. It was good to be home and let the events of the evening slowly sink in. The premiere had been a great success, and no one had shot them. That was two out of two.